Nick has always wanted Ame sister, but is he capable of ove come between them?

Amelia Fuller has been in love with her older brother's best friend for the better part of two decades. After working up the courage to finally tell him how she feels, he broke her heart. Now, three years later, she's home for the Christmas holidays and finds Nick's feelings toward her suddenly changed.

Nick doesn't like to make the same mistake twice. When Amelia arrives home after a three-year absence, Nick Kelly decides he's no longer going to hide the way he feels about her. His friendship with her brother and a past that left him feeling ashamed were the only things holding him back, but missing her for three long years has finally put things in perspective for Nick.

After Nick catches Amelia enjoying a little fetish pornography, he convinces her to agree to a hot fling, but much to Nick's displeasure, she wants to keep their affair secret. Sneaking around and indulging in risky sexual play while staying at her parent's home for the holidays won't get Amelia everything she's always dreamed of. Terrified to expose her heart once more, Amelia struggles to discover whether they can overcome their past.

My Mistletoe Master

Cover art by Angela Waters

ISBN: 978-1-4874-1048-3

Published by eXtasy Books Inc or
Devine Destinies, an imprint of eXtasy Books Inc
Look for us online at:
www.eXtasybooks.com or www.devinedestinies.com

My Mistletoe Master
Unexpected Changes
Book One

By

Cameron Allie

To Kerri,

Enjoy!

Cameron Allie xo

Dedication

For my mother and father, my sister and brother, and for my husband. Your support and love means the world.

Chapter One

Finally alone Amelia curled up in the family room, her laptop on the glass coffee table. Her dad had recently left for work and her mom had taken her brother Gabe to finish his Christmas shopping. Gabe always left it to the last few days. Amelia had only arrived home that morning; her exams had run late into the month, causing her to miss the beginning of the holidays. She'd only come home a few days ahead of her relatives who would soon be arriving at their custom-built country home for an extended stay.

Each year her grandparents, her aunt and uncle, and their three kids joined them for the holidays. Amelia's parents had established themselves years ago as the annual Christmas hosts. Their parties simply couldn't be beat, and the fact their extensive grounds could more than house all the family members certainly helped.

Taking this opportunity to enjoy the sanctuary of her childhood home before it became filled to the rafters, Amelia leaned over her laptop and opened the DVD driver to start the CD before she could change her mind. Sinking back into the couch, she waited for the videos to begin.

Amelia bit her lip in nervous anticipation as the first images flooded the screen. On the monitor, she watched as a man clad in black leather pants and nothing else restrained a woman. Slowly he raised one arm and then the other, locking them in place above her head. With her suspended from the ceiling, the man went about binding her feet to the floor. Naked and spread eagle, the woman moaned for the Dom. He denied her, slowly raking his hand over her exposed ass.

Growing wet between her legs, Amelia realized it had been too long since she'd had a man. Her body strained for more than her simple touch, but since she and her boyfriend had split two months ago, she'd just have to make do. To heighten her pleasure, she resisted her own needs, merely watching the two on the screen.

Amelia waited before she finally allowed herself to raise her own hand against her crotch. Pressing the palm of her hand against her jeans, she watched as the woman cried out in a mix of pain and pleasure as the man spanked her over and over. Moaning aloud with the video, Amelia abandoned her restraint, rocking against her hand. Her eyes drifted shut as she tugged on the button of her jeans, eager to touch herself, and begin working toward her climax.

A cough sounded behind her. She froze.

"What a great way to start my morning."

No longer alone, Amelia's eyes whipped open. She'd been so caught up in the moment, she never even heard him approach. Moving quickly, she slammed the lap top closed. With the sounds of the porno cut off, Amelia whirled around. Embarrassment crashed over her in waves as she found herself standing face to face with Nick, her brother's best friend.

She could feel his eyes on her as she gathered up her computer, hugging it to her chest. She peeked at him from behind her makeshift shield. Although she hadn't seen much of him in recent years, he could still take her breath away. His hair was sleep tousled, and he stood in nothing but his pajama bottoms. His broad chest was as bare as his feet, his expression dark and confused.

She realized he was waiting for an explanation. Instead, she went on the defensive. "What the hell are *you* doing here?"

He blinked. "I'm here for the holidays, like every year."

Amelia pressed a hand to her forehead. *Of course.*

"My mom didn't tell me you were here yet," she said lamely as though that explained her odd behaviour.

"Three days."

At a standstill, they merely stared each other down. What he thought of her in that moment, she didn't want to know. She could feel her cheeks heating and found herself wondering how long he had been standing there watching her.

Rounding the couch, she considered how many days she could hide in her room before her parents dragged her out. With any luck, she would manage to avoid Nick for a few days at the very least.

Aiming to shoulder her way past him so she could make a break for the stairs, Amelia put on a brave face and stalked toward him. His big body didn't budge as she tried to manoeuvre around him.

Attempting to edge by, she mumbled, "You know, maybe we could just forget about this. You know, pretend I'm just not here yet." She tried for a winning smile, but it faded when she saw humour light his eyes. Growing up, he and Gabe had teased her endlessly, and now she'd handed him ammunition.

"I don't think so." He took a step closer to her. She had to tilt her head to keep his gaze. Rascal that he was, he had the audacity to crack a smile at her discomfort. Her body was still primed for the orgasm she'd been denied. His nearness didn't help matters. Masculinity and dominance rolled off him. People took notice when he entered a room. He wasn't the broad and bulky type, but he was lean with a casual grace that made women think *stamina.*

"I can't believe it. Never would I have thought Gabe's little sister is such a perv."

She narrowed her eyes, convinced he was merely trying to get a rise out of her. Well, she'd shock him right back. "It's just a little kink."

His smile deepened. It worried her.

"I trust you won't tell anyone." She tried to keep the pleading out of her tone.

"What's it worth to you?"

This was the Nick she remembered from her childhood—rebel, tease, scoundrel. She gritted her teeth and insisted, "You won't tell."

"Well that depends on you, sweetheart."

Her gaze dropped to his mouth. Amelia fought the surge of butterflies that soared at his softly spoken words. "What do you want?"

Nick lifted his arm and clasped her chin between his fingers. She resisted the impulse to pull away, resisted the urge to moan at his soft touch. Her lips parted involuntarily when he stroked the pad of his thumb across her lower lip.

His hand dropped when the sound of a key turning in the lock echoed through the entranceway. About to be caught in a guilty moment for the second time, Amelia jumped away. A second later, her mom breezed in, all business with Gabe hot on her heels. "I can't believe you forgot your wallet."

Her brother shrugged.

"Gabe, we're going Christmas *shopping*. You need your wallet. Oh, Nick, good you're up," her mom said when she noticed them standing in the hallway. "Did you want to join us? Amelia's already done her shopping, but are there any last minute things you need?"

Nick expelled a pent up breath. His shoulders sagged. "Yeah, just give me a few minutes to get changed."

As quietly as he had emerged, Nick disappeared back through the door that led to the basement.

"Are you sure you don't want to come with us?" her mom

asked for the umpteenth time.

She nodded a little too fast. "Definitely."

"Come on, Gabe. Let's get a move on," her mother called up the stairs.

Gabe and Nick seemed to materialize at the same time. Amelia was amazed at the rapid transformation in Nick's appearance. Gone was his bed head, he'd replaced his pajamas with a dark wash pair of jeans. A black t-shirt was stretched over his muscled chest. Gabe vanished out the door after their mom, but Nick lingered, slipping on his running shoes. "Don't worry, Amelia, I won't say a word. But you can bet I'll be back to collect."

"Don't think too hard on it. Wouldn't want you to get a headache," she snipped.

He laughed at her attempted defiance. "It's all I'll be thinking about." He sent her a wink. "I'm sure you'll enjoy the rest of your morning."

Hoping to shock him, she snapped back, "Oh, I will."

Laughing, he closed the door between them.

* * * *

On a bench in the crowded mall, Nick sat with a nearly empty coffee cup dangling from his hand. The mall was packed with Christmas shoppers, hustling from store to store, weighted down with countless shopping bags. The smells from the food court wafted toward him from the hall, Asian noodles and burned popcorn. Somewhere nearby a child was crying amid the soft lull of conversation.

As he drained the last drops from the cup, he tried to use the caffeine boost to scrub the image of Amelia from his mind. She'd been touching herself. Watching porn and touching herself.

The little moaning noises she made kept echoing in his

head.

This was Gabe's baby sister he was thinking about. She was off limits. He couldn't touch her, he shouldn't even be thinking about her. Frustrated, his leg began tapping restlessly.

He'd wanted her for so long, but never could he do that to his best friend. If he had a sister, he'd do everything in his power to shelter her from men like himself. The worst part was he knew she wasn't indifferent to him.

Resting on the bench, unable to stop his fidgeting, Nick thought back to Christmas three years ago when she'd practically thrown herself at him. It had been awkward and so very tempting. She'd cornered him under the mistletoe, pressed her lithe body against him and brushed her lips over his. It had taken all of his self-restraint to walk away from her then. He didn't know if he could do it a second time.

This time she'd been flushed, her arousal clear on her delicate features. She might still be carrying a grudge from his rejection, but he knew that he could have her. If only he dared.

Seeing Gabe emerge from the shoe store with Sally, Nick rose from the bench, tossed the empty cup in the trash and headed toward them.

"So what else is on your list, Gabe?" Sally asked.

"I've got to get something for Paige—" Gabe consulted the list on his phone—"and you."

"Okay, well maybe we should split up for a little while then. I need to pick up a few things for work anyway." Her gaze swung to Nick. "You haven't done any shopping yet, Nick. What did you need to buy?"

He waved away her concern. "No, I'm pretty well done. I just came along for the ride. I might stop in the sports store before we head out."

She nodded. After looking at her watch, she suggested they meet at the food court in an hour. She trotted off toward the escalators.

Taking up a casual stride beside Gabe, the two headed off in the opposite direction. "So what stores do you need to visit?"

Gabe laughed. "I'm still not sure what to get my mom."

"Then maybe we should start with Paige's gift."

They wandered the halls of the mall, stopping in various stores, hunting for Sally Fuller's gift. As they passed *Victoria's Secret,* Nick couldn't help but wonder how Amelia might look in the blue lacy corset with the matching v-string panties that was fashioned on the mannequin in the window. Amelia was all curves and shapely legs. It would fit snuggly and, through the sheer bodice, he'd just be able to get a peek at her nipples. He struggled to rid himself of the image. Gulping down his guilt, Nick avoided Gabe's gaze.

When they came across a jewellery store, Gabe insisted that they stop. He picked out a necklace with a matching pair of earrings for his girlfriend Paige. They left the store to continue the search for Sally's gift.

"So Amelia was dating that guy," Nick said, trying for nonchalance, "... what was his name again?"

"Cody," Gabe answered, "but they broke up. Hey, let's try in here."

They turned into a crowded chocolate store and Gabe found the perfect basket of sweets for his mother. Standing in line for the checkout, Nick tried to pry more information out of Gabe. "Yeah, but that was a couple of months back. Why'd they break up?"

Gabe shrugged and said, "When it comes to relationships, Amelia and I have a don't-ask-don't-tell policy."

"Was he a jerk or something?"

Again Gabe shrugged. "Don't know. I never met the guy."

"How did that happen? They dated for like two years."

"She never brought him home. I guess it wasn't that

serious." Gabe rolled his shoulders with impatience as they neared the front of the line. "Why are you asking?" He slid Nick a pointed glare. "Why the sudden interest in Amelia's love life?"

Nick laughed and clapped his friend on the back. "Just don't want to say the wrong thing at dinner."

Gabe continued to eye him warily while he paid. Next, they strolled through the sporting goods store so that Nick could peruse some of the new merchandise. As a personal trainer, he liked to keep abreast of the newest advances in the market, but even as he searched through the shelves, he couldn't seem to tear his mind away from thoughts of Amelia.

She hadn't merely been watching a porno, she'd been watching a fetish porno. Was she into a little spanking, a little bondage? How far down that path had she travelled? Not knowing much about BDSM, he couldn't help but feel intrigued. He wanted to know more, and it all started with finding out just what made Amelia hot and heavy, and willing.

Chapter Two

Having finished blow-drying her hair, Amelia worked away at applying makeup. Rarely did she even bother with much, but for a night on the town with her girlfriends, she'd fancy up a bit. It was nice to have the house to herself before her relatives showed up, and with her family away at work, she could enjoy a nice long soak in the tub. She'd painted her nails and even thumbed through a magazine. All in all, it had been a relaxing day.

After being away so long, she was excited to spend time with her family, but with the term over and finals done, she needed a few days to unwind.

Fortunately, Nick was at work, too, and she didn't have to worry about his veiled threat to collect, whatever that had meant, or be concerned he was going to reveal her secret. After he'd disappeared out the door yesterday, Amelia had been too primed to do anything but hide away in her room and finish the deed she'd started in the family room. By then she hadn't needed the video. Knowing Nick was in the house and that he'd caught her was all the incentive she needed. She thought about his blue eyes and her knees went weak. She conjured up the image of his bare, smooth chest and bulging biceps and she got hopelessly wet between her legs. She'd pictured him stroking her with his rough hands and, in minutes, she was coming against her own hand, relieving, temporarily, the pressure in her aching body.

Dinner that night had been torture. The first family dinner she'd had in nearly a year and a half and she'd been able to do little more than shift uncomfortably in her chair, under Nick's smug stare. His smile mocked her. Each time he opened his mouth to speak, she feared he would blurt out her dirty secret. Instead, he had held on to it, goading it above her head. Burning with a horrid mixture of shame and want, she'd barely touched her food.

Having been crazy in love with him from the time she was six when Gabe brought him home from school and declared *this is my new best friend,* Amelia hated nothing more than being made a fool of in front of him. As children, she knew he'd always seen her as Gabe's silly little sister, but as they grew older, she could have sworn he'd been attracted to her. She hadn't developed early or quickly, but when the braces finally came off and her body realized it was time to discover the woman trapped inside, she had emerged victorious, and she'd been so sure he had noticed.

So sure in fact that three years ago she had laid it all on the line, offered herself up, and he had kicked her heart. Nothing in all her life had hurt as badly as that, not all the bullying she'd received as a pre-teen, not the time she'd broken her arm, not even when her high school boyfriend had dumped her for one of the girls from the cheer squad. Never had she felt so rejected and unattractive. She vowed she would forget all about Nick Kelly.

But now it was happening all over again. Ashamed and humiliated once more before the man of her dreams, Amelia didn't know how she could face him, how she could sit through another Christmas in complete heart-wrenching agony. Yet before he left to go shopping with her kin, she could have sworn it was interest that had prompted his words.

Don't do this to yourself, she thought as she applied the last of her makeup, attempting to plump up her lips with a final coat of lip-gloss.

Still toying with the idea of what to wear to dinner, Amelia explored her closet until a sharp knock sounded at her door. Frowning over her shoulder, she quickly donned her blue satin robe and tied the belt. She wondered who from her family would already be home.

In a rush to get rid of her caller in order to finish getting ready, Amelia merely opened the door a crack, hoping to discourage the person on the other side.

Impatiently she barked, "What?" but quickly widened her eyes in shock to see Nick standing before her. Still wearing his athletic livery from work, black cotton sweat pants, and a matching polo shirt pulled tight over his wide shoulders, Nick looked like the walking talking reason why any woman would actually *want* go to the gym.

Her heart beat quickened, but she fought for nonchalance, resting her cheek against the open door. She blinked at him and demanded again, "What?"

He planted his big hand on the door, shoving it open. "Geez is that always how you greet people?"

He breezed into her room full of arrogance. Amelia had to snap her jaw shut. He had never been in her room before. Growing up it had been off limits, forbidden.

His gaze wandered around her space, taking in the purple walls, her one bookshelf where she kept her Zen garden, few novels, and a smattering of magazines, her desk with the rollaway top where her laptop was nuzzled away, the vanity where her cosmetic things were strewn about, before finally coming to rest on her. She was suddenly very aware of her nakedness beneath the robe.

Drawing herself up, she stood by the door and gestured for him to leave. "I'm getting ready to go out."

"I want to talk to you."

Frustrated, Amelia let out a sigh. He wasn't going to budge, not until he got what he wanted. Once again, she resumed her seat before the vanity and began rummaging through her jewellery box. It was so much harder to pick jewellery when she didn't yet know what she'd be wearing, but she needed something to distract herself from looking at Nick. *In her room.*

A second later, she heard the door close. Looking up, she saw he'd shut the door and was now leaning against it. Trapped with him, she should have felt threatened, should have felt imposed upon, but instead she had to fight the pull of her body, the tightening ache of her pussy.

She licked her suddenly dry lips, which only drew his gaze. She could see the slight rise and fall of his chest as he drew in each breath, carefully planning out whatever it was he had come to say. She wanted to see him straining for breath as he rode deep between her legs. Embarrassed by her train of thought, Amelia nearly looked away. She wrestled to keep his gaze, unwilling to let him know how he still affected her.

Finally, he broke the silence. "Do you always get off to videos with people being spanked?"

Exasperated, Amelia turned away. "Oh my god! Will you drop it already? Just leave me alone." She shot him a dirty look.

Pushing away from the door, he crossed the room in two giant strides. She had to strain her neck to look up at where he loomed over her. He'd always been a tall man. He seemed almost angry with her when he demanded, "Is it always spanking? Is it bondage? Or is it sometimes something lighter? Was it just porn or is this some fetish thing you have going on?"

Outraged, Amelia tried to surge out of her seat, but with his hands on her shoulders, Nick forced her back down onto the bench.

What right did he have to demand to know her preferences?

Angry at his self-assurance, she struggled in his grasp. Physically bested, Amelia slumped in her seat. It wasn't until then that she felt the little circular pattern that his thumbs were teasing into her shoulder. He was touching her. Why was he touching her? Why was he asking her such questions?

"Amelia." This time his voice was soft.

She looked up into the mirror. His gaze was also fixed on the mirror. Glancing down, she realized her dressing gown had come open along the centre. The valley between her breasts lay naked, the curves of her breasts barely covered. Her navel jewellery winked at them before the blue robe pulled tight just before the waist. Drawing in a breath, she realized it hadn't been anger she'd seen in Nick's eyes. It had been lust.

Somehow, somewhere along the way, she had captured his attention, and it seemed now he was wondering what she was going to do with it.

She and Cody had indulged in a little bondage play, but when she had hinted at something more, Cody had been appalled. He hadn't wanted to keep pace with her. Now she wondered if Nick just might be the man for the position. He was strong and confident, he'd make an excellent Dom, she thought. But would he ever go for that sort of a thing?

Nick was on the lure, but Amelia wondered if she should dare take the chance and tell him her deepest desire. She bit her lip as she studied him in the mirror. If she reached out to him, he held the power to destroy her still fragile heart. Or she could get everything her body and soul craved.

She wanted to close her eyes, to soak in the pleasure of his light caress, but she didn't dare miss the chance to watch his face as he touched her. His fingers drummed over her throat, pausing on her artery. She wondered if he could feel her excitement, could smell her arousal. She badly wanted to ask, *Why now? What's changed?* but she didn't dare. Instead, she decided to risk it all. "It's more."

With his thumbs, he pushed her chin up, forcing her to look at him. He leaned down, inching ever closer to her mouth. "Pardon?"

"It-it's more. I guess... I guess it's a fetish." She couldn't help the stutter that suddenly spilled out. With closed eyes, she cursed herself for being a coward.

His lips skimmed her cheek, making her draw a quick inhale. It was insane how quickly he stirred her blood. He hadn't kissed her, he hadn't even touched her, not really, and yet the yearning she felt for him consumed her being.

"Tell me what you want," he demanded.

She paused, fighting herself.

"Amelia." Roughly, he pulled his fingers through her hair, dragging her head even further backward. "I need to know what it is you want."

The words tumbled from her mouth. "I want to completely give up control. I'm a submissive at heart." Her lashes swept open. She stared fiercely up at him. "I want you to tell me what to do. Tell me what I want. I want you to make me beg for you."

She saw how her words affected him. His jaw locked, his nostrils flared. For a heartbeat, he didn't speak, but she was no longer afraid.

"Good answer," he said at last.

His fingers released her hair, his hands dropping to part her satin robe. With tantalizing slowness, he bared her upper body, her breasts full and round, her nipples pulled taut from their heated exchange. She badly wanted him to touch her. He waited until her gaze met his in the mirror before his warm adept fingers slipped down cupping, her weight in his palms. His forefinger and thumb came up to draw circles round and round her nipples. When she moaned, he tweaked them, pinching hard. Biting her lip, she dropped her head back against the hard wall of his abdomen. Moisture pooled between her thighs.

"That's a good girl."

After a few more minutes of his playing with her tits, he stopped and pulled the material back up over her shoulders. She looked at him in question.

"Go lay on the bed."

Standing, she asked, "How do you want me?"

Grasping her chin, he forced her to look up. He was searching her face for something. Fear? Confusion? Arousal?

"Too many ways," he whispered before he kissed her. Gently his lips brushed hers, but when she reached for him, slipping her tongue along his lower lip, he gave himself over completely. Opening his mouth hungrily, he nearly bruised her lips with his crushing need. When his teeth clashed against hers, he backed off a bit, his tongue still searching her mouth, greedily taking everything she was willing to offer.

Finally able to touch him, Amelia ran her fingers over the muscles of his stomach and carved chest. At her simple touch, he groaned and pulled her closer, his left hand cupping her jaw while his right parted the robe once more. Unwilling to try to temper his response, Amelia struggled to keep up. His hand slipped down over the left cheek of her ass and hauled her against his body. She rocked against him, succumbing to his rhythm. She revelled in the feel of his erection against her bare flesh. Through the cotton of his pants, his hard dick stroked the warmth of her core. She ground against him, moaning helplessly.

He tore his mouth away with a ragged growl. "Oh, fuck."

Both panting for breath, lips wet and stinging, Amelia waited for him to do something.

"On the bed. On your back. Now."

Compliant, she did just that, unaware that as she passed him he pulled the sash from the loops on her robe's belt.

The air cooled her and the sexual fog lifted slightly. As she lay down, she arranged the robe to cover her body from his view. At the edge of the bed, he studied her. Resting one knee on the mattress, Nick reached for the robe to bare her once more.

"Nick." More modest than a moment ago, she touched his wrist.

A smile lit the corners of his mouth. He lowered his body atop hers and once more took her mouth, this time in a gentle caress. Enjoying his light kisses, Amelia melted once more under his mastery. His hands ran down the length of her arms, interlocking their fingers. Amelia relished the feeling of simply holding hands with Nick Kelly, but when he raised her arms up over her head, the full realization of what she'd gotten herself into hit her.

She had given Nick carte blanche when it came to her body and, as she felt him binding her wrists to the headboard, she realized, wickedly, that she didn't care. This time it would be different. This man knew what he was doing.

* * * *

Nick had no idea was he was doing. Making it up as he went along, Nick tugged on the satin bindings and, satisfied with his handiwork, rolled onto his side. Her beauty nearly stole his breath away. Her long brown tresses fanned out across her pillow, the blue satin illuminating the heat in her innocent blue eyes. He licked his lip as his gaze raked her body.

Impatient as ever, Amelia's legs shifted, drawing against each other in anticipation.

With her suitably restrained, Nick took his time pulling back the edges of the robe. He looked her over, took in her rosy nipples, her full breasts, her slim tummy. His stare stopped at the apex of her thighs, taking in the light dusting of dark curls. No longer able to resist, he reached out, running his fingers over the delicate flesh of her legs. He skimmed the expanse of her thighs, leisurely moving downward stopping near her knee. The polish on her toes matched the polish on her fingernails. Nick smiled, barely able to pick a place to start.

He knew he didn't have long, but in this moment, he wanted to give her pleasure. He didn't want to rush into sex with Amelia. He was past the point of turning back, but his knowledge on BDSM was lacking. He needed to learn more before he took her to bed. The last thing he wanted to do was disappoint her. But right now he knew exactly what she needed.

He could feel her gaze on his face yet forced himself to ignore it. If he looked at her, he'd want her even more and, as it was, his dick was standing at full attention. Struggling to keep his awareness on his movements, he murmured, "Open your legs."

Slowly she inched her thighs apart.

Stroking up her legs, he brushed his palms against her hips, deliberately skirting her mound. He fondled her tits for a moment before lowering his head and drawing one stiff nipple into his mouth. Beneath him, she moaned and bucked. With his arm across her midriff, he forced her to be still and take it. When he switched to her other nipple, he could feel her pulling against her restraints, no doubt wanting to touch him. *All in good time,* he thought as he feasted upon her at his leisure.

"Nick," she cried, thrashing her head against the pillow, "please."

With a dark grin, he drew back and once more let his hand travel down her gorgeous body. He teased the sensitive skin on the inside of her thighs, inching ever nearer. She struggled, wanting him to put his hand to her pussy.

Nick tossed a few of the frilly throw pillows from the bed before bending his elbow so he could prop his head against his hand. Relaxing on his side, his entire focus was on her face. She closed her eyes, fighting the sensations that racked her body, and bit her lower lip. He let a few of her pubic hairs curl around his finger, toying with her softness, before finally dipping his finger into her waiting folds. He groaned when he found her already wet.

"Amelia." Sinking closer to her body, he skimmed his nose across her cheek as he played with her. Carefully slipping his fingers over her pussy lips, he tested her, discovering how she liked to be touched. When he found her little clitoris, she rewarded him by turning her face, searching for his lips to kiss.

His tongue rubbed rhythmically against hers, while lower he rubbed her wetness over her pulsing flesh. Knowing she wanted more, he deliberately pushed one finger into her passage.

Slowly at first, he worked his finger in and out of her tight pussy, watching her face for any sign of discomfort, but all he saw was pleasure. Her lips parted on an exhale as she enjoyed his every stroke. Her body rocked with him as he quickened his pace, adding a second digit, finger fucking her harder with each probe until she teetered on the edge.

Intent on pushing her to a climax, he brought his thumb up to press against her clit. Then her phone buzzed.

They both paused to look at her nightstand where her phone was lit up and vibrating. Amelia pulled her brows together and struggled again against her restraints. Laughing at her effort, Nick reached across her naked body to snatch the phone off the table.

"It's Amy," he said, looking at the screen.

She must have read his mischievous smile. Urgently she told him, "No, Nick, no."

Nick flexed his fingers inside of her, her body clenched against him as she fought not to moan. With his other hand, he slid his finger over the screen, answering the call.

He raised it to his ear. "Hello."

Confused, Amy asked, "Who is this?"

As though it were totally natural for him to be answering her phone, he replied, "Nick."

"Where's Amelia? We're waiting out front."

Nick eyed the naked woman before him, twisting his fingers again touching that magical spot inside. Amelia gasped and mouthed, *Stop that!*

"She's right here," he countered. "She's just getting ready to *come*—" she glared up at him but he continued—"outside. I think she's still got to get dressed, though."

"Why did you answer her phone?"

Nick avoided that question, "She'll be down in five."

After hanging up the phone, Nick gave Amelia a quick kiss on the tip of her cute nose. It was mean he knew, but he shoved off the bed and untied her hands. "You'd best get ready. Sounds like they have been waiting for you for a bit," he scolded.

Closing the robe, she skidded over to the edge of the bed. "You're going to leave me like this?"

He came back to the bedside. "Why should you be any less on edge than me?" Taking her hand, he pressed it against his straining erection. Yeah, he'd had every intention of giving her a mind blowing orgasm, but for some reason it excited him terribly to know she'd spend her night thinking about him, wet and waiting for him.

She stroked him twice before he brought her hand up to kiss her palm. He wanted her to be ready for him when the time came. He pulled her into his arms, urging her body against his. "I want you to think about me tonight. Don't you dare sneak off to the bathroom to help yourself." To ensure she understood, he cupped his hand over her mound, pressing the robe against her wet thighs. "I want you hot and bothered when you come home to me. Is that clear?"

Weakly, she nodded against his chest. Content, he strode to the door. If he didn't walk away soon she'd never make it down to her friends. Besides, he thought as he stepped into the hallway, closing the door between them, he had a lot of research to do.

Chapter Three

Relishing the cool December chill that clung on the air, Amelia curled her gloved fingers over the door handle of the back seat. A gust of wind whipped against her cheeks, making her sigh with the relief it brought her flushed skin. What had Nick done to her? Her skin was heated; her cheeks blush red, her legs wobbled beneath her and her pussy was still aching with the desperate need for release. She was shocked by her own behaviour, unsure of how she'd let it go from zero to a hundred so quickly.

She opened the door and sank into the cushioned seat. The thick heat from the warmed vehicle nearly took her breath away.

"Finally!" Geneva said from the other end of the back seat. "What took you so long?"

Three sets of eyes gawked at her. Lynn peered over the front passenger seat, while Amy bent her arm over her headrest and swivelled from the driver seat to have a look at her. "Why did Nick answer your phone?"

Amelia couldn't stop the flush that rushed into her cheeks.

"Amy, you were right!" Lynn squealed. "They are sleeping together."

Amelia's brows pulled tight together. "I was just busy, getting ready to meet you guys."

"We said six." Amy glanced at the dashboard. "It's nearly six-thirty."

"So let's get going then." Amelia fastened her seatbelt.

Geneva leaned closer, examining her. She sat back with a

satisfied smirk. "No, they're not fucking."

Not yet, the words nearly slipped out of her mouth, but Amelia bit her lip to keep from uttering them. She didn't know what was going on between her and Nick, but the last thing she needed was Geneva turning into a jealous bitch. There had always been something about Geneva that kept Amelia closed off. Geneva was beautiful and knew it, she enjoyed her blatant sexually, but what really bothered Amelia was how Geneva never missed an opportunity to put any of them down, to criticize and bully them. Lynn normally bore the brunt of it.

As Amy put the car in gear and pulled away from the curb, Geneva started to pull her usual bullshit. "He didn't want you three years ago." Geneva's glance flicked over her. "You haven't changed, so why would he be interested now?"

"Shut up."

"You threw yourself at him and he didn't want you."

God, how Geneva's words cut through her, rehashing her shame. Amelia fought to ignore her. Bullies wanted to get a rise out of you.

"I still can't believe you did it. And under the mistletoe, how..." Geneva paused, emphasizing her point, "... *pathetic.* It must have broken your heart to be left standing there all alone."

From the front seat, Lynn snickered. But without a reaction from Amelia, Geneva changed tactics.

"I almost had him once." She flicked her hair over her shoulder and stared out the window. "But I changed my mind at the last minute."

Not believing a word of that, Amy snorted. It was nice to have at least one ally in the car.

Geneva ignored her. "He's not really my type."

"Not your type?" Amelia scorned, "You don't like tall, handsome, built..."

"Whatever." Geneva shrugged, and then she leaned closer as though telling Amelia a secret, even though she blurted it out loud enough for all to hear. "He is really well hung."

Before Amelia could respond, Amy interrupted. "It feels like a margarita night. Who's in?"

Soon enough they'd all agreed and Amy managed to change the topic from Nick to what their plans were for the holidays. Although they were no longer discussing Nick, the thought of him never fully left Amelia's mind. She still couldn't get over the *why*. As Geneva had pointed out, nothing had changed so why all of a sudden was Nick ready to get things started between them. No matter what the girls talked about, she couldn't stop from wondering. When she got back home, did Nick expect them to pick up where they'd left off?

Once the car was parked outside the restaurant, they all ambled out into the cold before heading over to the building. Nearing seven o'clock, they had missed their reservations, but fortunately, because it was a Tuesday, the dinner rush was slowing down and they only had to wait at the bar for fifteen minutes before their table was ready. Lynn, Amy and Amelia all glanced over the menu while waiting for Geneva to cease flirting with the bartender to join them. Soon they had all ordered and with the exception of Amy, they were on their second margarita.

"Do you think it would be okay with your parents if my new boyfriend came to the Christmas party?" Lynn asked gleefully. It was her first boyfriend and they had all been thrilled for her. Amelia was the only one who had yet to meet him. Lynn seemed to glow from his attentions and Amelia couldn't be happier for her.

"Of course he can come. My mom always plans for more people," Amelia assured her.

The Fuller's annual Christmas party was a huge event that

pulled in a crowd of over two hundred and each year it grew in size. Her mother was a party planner and her father owned a construction company. It had started as a party to help his business grow, but as the years continued and both her parents flourished in their fields, the party became a big hit in the town. It had grown so large that ten years ago her parents had taken to renting out the manor house to accommodate the crowd. Now her mother hired caterers, valets, a disc jockey, and a cleanup crew, among countless other paid staff. It was invitation only. Off-duty police officers checked invitations and IDs at the door. Taxi drivers waited at the end of the night to ferry the drunks to their homes.

It was at the Fuller's party three years ago that Amelia had made a fool of herself over Nick. Left stranded under the mistletoe, Amelia had pledged not to come back home until she had healed her broken heart. She would bring home a boyfriend to rub in Nick's face.

That hadn't gone well. She'd dated Cody for over two years, but never felt right bringing him home. She'd avoided Christmas, but this year she'd told her mother to send Cody an invitation. Then she'd gone and dumped him.

Their waitress brought out their food.

"Text me his first and last name and I'll make sure he's on the list."

Lynn beamed, grabbed her phone and punched in the information. "Thanks."

"No problem," Amelia replied as her phone buzzed against her hip. "I can't wait to meet him."

"So you coming home this year, does that mean you're finally over Nick?" Geneva spun her fork in her spaghetti. Amelia frowned, but before she could reply, Geneva surprised her. "I only ask because it's been rather dull without you. We missed you."

Amelia's jaw went slack at the other woman's comment.

Amy and Lynn agreed.

"I know you've come home a few times," Geneva continued, "but you never stay very long and Christmas hasn't been the same without you."

It took her a minute to recover. "Thanks, Gen."

"Yeah," Lynn wondered, "when are you coming back?"

"School will be done in April. I'm going to move back then." The girls squealed their delight. "I've already got a job lined up with my mom. I'll be staying with my parents until I figure out where I want to live."

"Ooooh, that's exciting." Geneva seemed genuinely happy.

Amelia turned her attention to Amy. "Tell me about this new house that you and Brent are moving into. When will it be done?"

"In the summer!" Amy pulled out the floor plan for Amelia's sake, but all four of them pored over it, giving her decorating ideas and discussing the benefits of that particular model. "Your dad gave us a great deal."

After their meal was done, they ordered two desserts to split among the table. Before they arrived, Amelia excused herself to go to the restroom. Amy shoved out of the booth to go with her. As they washed their hands and reapplied their lipstick, Amy kept sneaking glances at Amelia.

"What is it?" Amelia asked as she removed a stray hair from her eyes.

"You're sleeping with Nick."

It wasn't a question. Amelia and Amy had been best friends long before Lynn and Geneva joined their company. They trusted each other completely.

"We're not sleeping together."

"Come on. This is me you're talking to now. Spill it."

"We have not slept together, *yet*."

Amy shifted, resting her hips on the counter. "Now we're getting somewhere. Haven't slept together, *yet*."

"Yet." Amelia couldn't hide her grin.

"I knew it! Give me some details, girl. Why the heck did he pick up your phone? Nearly gave me a heart attack when he answered. What's going on?"

Amelia stumbled over that question. "I really don't know."

"Does he like you?"

At a loss, Amelia shrugged. "I really don't know. We started fooling around before you called. I don't know where it was going, but I don't think it's over yet."

Amy practically squealed with glee. "We should have a code word for stuff like this. Next time say like panther or something and I'll know to just leave you be."

They laughed. "Come on we should get back out there. And not a word," Amelia warned as she pulled on the bathroom door.

Amy stopped her with a hand on her elbow. "Amelia. I'm happy for you, I really am. But be careful with him. I know what he did to you all those years ago, how badly you've wanted him. But try not to let him hurt you."

She knew her friend's heart was in the right place. Amelia patted Amy's hand. "I'll be sure to be safe."

Later that night, Amelia was the last to be dropped off. As she pushed open the door to her house, her phone vibrated. The text was from Amy. *Is he a good kisser?*

In the process of texting back, Amelia's attention was torn away from her phone by a very familiar laugh. She left the entrance and wandered into the kitchen. At the centre island, Gabe and Nick were playing cards. Nick had his back to her, but Gabe looked up when she came into the room. Before tucking away her phone, she checked the time.

Eleven-thirty. Not terribly late, but not that early. Was Nick waiting up for her? Did he want to pick up where they left off? For that matter, did she?

"Hey," Gabe said, "you're home early. First night out with

the girls I thought you'd hit up a club or something."

At her brother's welcome, Nick turned in his seat. He slung his arm over the back of his chair, but said nothing.

Amelia tried to ignore Nick's burning stare. She laughed at her brother. "It's a Tuesday night."

"So?"

No doubt if they'd been a bunch of guys that'd have gone to the 'rippers, despite it being a Tuesday. Amelia shook her head. "No, we just had dinner and drinks."

Gabe went to the fridge to refill his beverage.

"Got hammered, did ya?" Nick's lazy smile made her heart flutter.

She glowered at him. "No."

"Nick, you want something?"

"Yeah, water, thanks." He swung his gaze over to Gabe and caught the bottle of water that was tossed at him.

Shuffling awkwardly in the doorway, Amelia didn't know how to proceed. No way would they let Gabe know what had transpired between them, but Amelia had no clue as to what Nick wanted from her, and with her brother there, it seemed she wouldn't find out.

As Gabe disappeared from view to reach for a soda from the bottom of the fridge, Nick pointed at her. Then he pointed down, to the basement. *Meet me downstairs,* he mouthed.

Frozen in the doorway, she didn't have time to respond. Behind the fridge door, Gabe straightened. "Want us to deal you in the next hand?"

She considered it for a moment. "No." She faked a yawn. "I'm going to head to bed."

Nick frowned.

"Suit yourself." Gabe resumed his place at the counter.

Amelia gave them a little wave before ducking out of the room. "See you *both* in the morning."

No doubt Nick would fume over that. *Let him stew,* she

thought. She had enjoyed the last twenty-four hours with him, but he'd never been clear about what was happening. She'd spilled out her deepest secret, now it was his turn to do the talking, his turn to admit what he wanted.

As she sauntered down the hallway, she heard her brother say, "Remember the days she used to bug the hell out of us to let her play with us?"

She missed Nick's response as her cell phone started ringing. Cody's name flashed over the screen. She let it go to voice mail. By the time she reached her bedroom, she'd gotten a text message.

Why won't you answer my calls? I've reconsidered. I want to be with you. Call me.

They'd been over it so many times in the last few weeks. Suddenly he'd changed his mind. Try as he may to get back together, she'd have no part of it. Angry, she shut her phone off and hooked it up to the charger. Any other calls or texts from her ex would have to wait until tomorrow. She refused to let him plague her through the night.

Thrusting the thought of Cody from her mind, Amelia focused all her attention on thoughts of Nick.

Chapter Four

Clark Griswold ranted on screen. Gabe and Paige laughed at Chevy Chase's antics.

Nick lounged in the armchair, trying to keep his focus on the Christmas comedy. He failed. His gaze kept slipping to where Amelia sat curled up on the love seat parallel to the sofa that Gabe and Paige cuddled on.

He'd waited up half the night, expecting Amelia to come downstairs to be with him. Overtired, he'd sent her a few texts she hadn't responded to. When the morning had come, she sent him one text, *Sorry my phone was off.* As if that explained it!

Frustrated and exhausted, Nick had gone to the gym early in an effort to overcome his irritation. It hadn't worked. He just didn't understand it. Amelia had seemed so ready, so willing, but then she'd skipped out on him. He was sure she wanted him, why was she suddenly so shy?

In the darkened basement, he contemplated her. She slipped one socked foot beneath her bottom, and wrapped her arms around a throw pillow that she'd cuddled into her lap. She looked so soft and innocent, but he knew a fire burned behind that façade.

She must have felt his stare. She turned her face away from the screen. Capturing her gaze, Nick narrowed his eyes. Her breath caught. The scent of her shampoo carried to him across the small space.

He sent her a wink that must have shocked her. Nick fought not to laugh when she glued her eyes back to the screen. Oh yes, she wanted him, he had no doubts. The way she suddenly began petting the pillow gave her away.

He directed his attention back to the television and, for a while, managed to get back into the film. Then movement caught his eye, and sure enough, Gabe had pulled Paige into his arms and was giving her a slow passionate kiss.

Paige shocked him. It had surprised the whole family when Gabe brought home the new preacher's daughter. She'd been so demure around his parents, she was prim and proper whenever they were out in public, but Nick was beginning to wonder if it was all a charade. For a preacher's daughter, she laughed a little too loudly when Griswold let out fowl curses. At first, Nick thought it had made her uncomfortable, but now the way she melted against Gabe had him second-guessing his first impression of Little Miss Church-Goer.

As Paige shifted and their kiss got a little too heated for company, Nick saw the moment wasn't lost on Amelia. "Ew, Gabe, god, get a room!"

Paige and Gabe tore apart with a soft gasp. With a smirk, Gabe glanced at his sister. "Hey, Nick, your bed is empty, mind if we..."

Laughing, Nick reached toward Amelia, his fingers grazing her pant leg. "Pass me that pillow, would you? I've got to suffocate your brother."

Amelia recoiled from his light touch as Paige pinched Gabe for his jest.

"Ow, damn it woman that hurt."

Paige gave him a saucy smile before settling back to watch the movie.

It wasn't long after that the film came to a close and the credits rolled across the screen. Gabe stretched out his long arms and Paige yawned.

"Not a bad movie," Gabe commented.

"Just as funny every year," Nick agreed.

"Well, I should really get Paige home." Gabe ushered his girlfriend to the bottom of the staircase. Amelia rose as well, no doubt trying to avoid being left alone with him.

"Wait up! I'm coming up, too."

Stretching his leg out, Nick barred her exit. Trapped between the couches, Amelia glared at him. "Stay, play a round with me." He nodded toward the ping-pong table.

Hands on her hips, she considered him. He could see her fighting with herself. She knew what would happen if she stayed, and she knew given the chance she should leave. With his back to Gabe, he offered her a slow smile, his eyes silently commanding her to stay. They both knew she wasn't going anywhere.

"You're not tired?"

"Not at all."

She stood toying with the idea. Gabe was probably wondering why she was stalling, but soon the choice was taken away from her. Paige yawned.

"Look," Gabe said, "we got to go. Paige has to work early. Have a good night." The two ascended the stairs, leaving Nick alone with Amelia.

They both seemed to hold their breath as they waited to hear the door at the top of the stairs shut.

Nick checked the impulse to drag her into his arms. Instead, he pushed out of the armchair and sauntered over to the ping-pong table. Slowly, deliberately he picked up one of the paddles, his stare never leaving her face. Her gaze followed his actions, but she didn't dare move.

He spun the paddle on its head. "You always sucked at this game."

That snapped her into action. "I do not suck."

"Oh, I bet you do." He tossed the second paddle to her.

She threw it back onto the table. "I don't want to play." She headed for the stairs.

Nick panicked. "Chicken."

She turned on him. "What do I get if I win?"

"You won't win." He couldn't keep the smugness out of his voice. Her gaze flicked from him to the paddle, stalling. "Winner picks their prize."

She walked to the table and lifted the paddle. "Fine."

He lobbed the ball at her. "Ladies serve first."

It wasn't long after that Amelia lost by four points. She hurled the paddle down. "Damn."

Nick smiled wolfishly at her. "I win."

She stiffened as he rounded the table, no doubt wondering if she could out run him. There was nowhere she could hide from him. His fingers raked over the flesh of her arm as he encircled her, trapping her body. His hands brushed against hers where they rested on the edge of the table. With her back pressed against his front, he felt the shudder that swept through her body.

"What do you want?" she asked weakly, not daring to look at him.

His lips skimmed her ear. "My prize." Brushing her hair back from her neck, he kissed the tender spot where her shoulder met her neck. "You'll do *exactly* as I say."

From here, he had a great view of her breasts, pressed up and nearly tumbling from her purple tank top. He longed to touch them again. Instead, he settled his hands firmly on her hips, his big fingers nearly spanning her midriff. He hauled her luscious ass up against his groin.

"Why did you avoid me last night?"

She tried to squirm free, but his grip was tight. The way her ass rubbed against his jeans only got him more excited, and from the way her breath caught, he was sure it did the same for her. "I didn't. You were playing cards with Gabe. I didn't want to interrupt."

"You hid in your room."

"I was tired."

"Oh no," he growled hotly into her ear, "you'll have to do better than that."

She drew in a breath. "I wasn't sure you wanted this."

Laughing, he rubbed his erection against her ass. "Is that what you *really* think?"

"No," she muttered as she ground against him.

It would be so easy to take her now. To bend her over the table and fuck her from behind, and god how he wanted to, but not for their first time.

"I've been thinking about what you said yesterday, about what you want." He felt her tense beneath him. Snaking his hands up her flat tummy, he cupped her breasts in his hands before pulling her upright so her back was flush with his chest. Pressing his nose in her hair, he breathed in the scent of coconut. "I'm inclined to give it to you."

Keeping one hand moulded over her breast, he slipped the other down her front until he cupped her sex. He could feel her heat through her jeans. She was so *fucking* hot, and he didn't doubt she was just as wet.

She tried to move against his hand, but he anchored her in place. "For someone who claims to be a sub, you certainly don't act like it."

"Nick, *please,*" she moaned, writhing against him.

He tapped her mound, once, twice, until finally she dropped her head against his shoulder and whispered, "What would you have me do?"

"That's much better, compliance." They needed to set boundaries, guidelines. And they would soon enough, but tonight he wanted to explore their sudden passion. "First, we have a problem. You stood me up last night."

She went still. "We never made definitive plans."

He laughed at her attempt to explain her disappearing act last night. "You knew full well that I expected a repeat performance. You disobeyed me." Boldly reaching across to the table, he methodically picked up the paddle once more. Where his hand lay on her chest, he felt her breathing become faster, her heartbeat quickening. "That can't happen."

She twisted her head to look at him. "What? You're going to spank me? Punish me?" She mocked him, and he realized she was expecting him to back down.

Raising his hand further up her chest, Nick grabbed hold of her chin, forcing her gaze away from him. He kissed the corner of her mouth, her cheek. He lightly tongued, and then bit her earlobe. "We're going to have so much fun, you and I, just as soon as you learn to obey me, to do as I say, when I say it."

She shivered against him. He'd never really given a second thought to BDSM before this, before Amelia, but now it revved him up. The thought of her obeying his every word, his every command, the thought of making Gabe's little sister sink down on her knees to suck his cock...

But he was getting ahead of himself.

Holding her body firmly against him, he used the edge of the paddle to trace up her stomach, circling each breast. "Do you really think you should have kept me waiting last night?"

With one hand on her throat, he felt her swallow, felt each ragged breath as he waited for her answer.

"No."

"That's right. You should have come downstairs to me, and let me finger fuck you until you were raw, until you begged me for more. And then maybe I would have given it to you."

She moaned. He wasn't sure if it was his words that ripped the sound from her mouth or the wooden paddle catching on her tight nipple.

"We ought to teach you a lesson." He suddenly released his hold on her, and she swaggered, unsteady on her own legs. "Lean over, and brace your hands on the table."

She did as he asked, bending over, leaving herself exposed.

Feeling a bit like a jerk, but knowing she'd love it he said, "Open your legs a bit, widen your stance for me."

She shifted her feet a little further apart. With her head hanging between her arms, she looked at him from the corner of her eye. He merely sent her a jaded little smile, before making a show of examining her open position. He ran his free hand up the inside of her thigh and over her ass, cupping and cradling, and hefting first one cheek then the other. "Perfect."

Next, he smoothed the paddle over the little heart that was embroidered on her back pocket. He brought the paddle back. Amelia's face was shaded by her loose hair, but he knew she was waiting for him to spank her with it.

He paused.

The only problem was that once he struck her delicate skin there was no turning back from such an act. He dined at the same table as her parents, he enjoyed their hospitality. He was best friends with her brother. Could he really debase Mr. and Mrs. Fuller's daughter, right here in their basement?

He brought the paddle down hard on her delectable ass.

* * * *

At the first sharp sting of the paddle, Amelia jumped. Knowing he couldn't see her face, she smiled to herself. He'd actually done it. He'd pretty well said he'd accept her as his submissive. The way he touched her, the brazen things he said had her beyond ready for him.

The paddle came down again.

Nick was so much more forceful than Cody had ever been, so sure of himself.

Again.

Amelia bit her lip to keep the wild groan from exploding

from her lips. She loved being at his mercy, she wanted to accept his punishment. Her ass began to sting from the wooden slaps.

He spanked her again, and she had no doubt her ass would be red.

Once more, he struck her before tossing the paddle back onto the table. Silence filled the room, the only sound was his ragged breathing. He was new to this, she knew, probably unsure of what to do next, unsure if he'd hurt her. Little did he know that he'd done nothing but please her.

"Amelia?" he questioned, doubt lining his voice.

She didn't move a muscle. "Yes."

The triumph in her tone must have appeased him. "Do you understand what you did wrong?"

Her pussy throbbed in response to his gentle mockery. Haughtily, she looked over her shoulder at him, tossing her thick hair aside. "Yes, Sir."

Hunger leaped into his eyes. "Come here."

She left her bent position and quickly crossed the space between them. She'd half expected him to gather her close and kiss her, but with causal familiarity, he reached behind her and smoothed his hands over her still stinging behind.

"How's your sweet little tush?"

Rather than answer, she leaned forward to lip at his chin. Deliberately keeping his mouth away, Nick continued to taunt her as he slipped his nimble fingers beneath the tight material of her jeans. She almost winced as his hands travelled over the smarting cheeks, but she soon forgot her pain when he followed the line of her thong. He tugged upward, causing the material to chafe, wedging her. Lower, the material pulled tight against her inflamed vulva.

Such simple actions and the man drove her mad. She moaned her response. "Nick, please."

He leaned down and kissed her, tonguing her deeply. He

swirled his tongue around hers and she tasted the whiskey that he'd drank earlier. Her mouth opened wide to accept him. She sucked lightly on his tongue. When she relented, he nipped at her, gently biting her lower lip. He ushered her backward with him, never leaving her mouth. She gladly reciprocated, kissing him all the while as he drew her away from the lighted ping-pong table, into the darkened television area. The screen was off and the dim pot lights overhead generated limited light. They sunk into the secluded space. Nick leaned back against the bar railing as he brought their make out session to a close.

"You are so *fucking* delicious." He licked his lips. "I can't wait to taste all of you."

She shuddered.

Gathering her close once more, he nuzzled her neck, giving her an open-mouthed kiss. For a moment, she wondered if he'd leave her marked, but soon realized she didn't care. She could hide a hickey easily enough, but she certainly didn't want him to stop. At length, he kissed his way up to her ear. He tucked a few strands of hair behind it.

She pressed her body against his, ready to do anything he asked of her. When he ran his fingertip along her lower lip, she knew he intended to kiss her again, but as he leaned toward her, she foiled his plans. Parting her lips, she drew his finger into her mouth.

Closing her eyes, she sucked on his finger, his sharp intake of breath only spurring her on further.

Lightly she encircled the tip of his large finger with the edge of her tongue, before gradually tugging it further into her mouth. She sucked on it, pressing his short well-kept nail against the roof of her mouth. Her cheeks pinched inward as she created a vacuum-like suction to cradle his finger.

He continued to test her, pushing his middle finger further into her mouth, until she took all of it. He pulled it out only to press it back in, building a sensual rhythm. She made a happy noise deep in her throat, thinking about how badly she wanted more than just his finger.

Retracting it, he used the wet tip to liberally dampen her lips. It only excited her more.

"I want you on your knees. I want you to suck me off."

Desire licked through her veins at his command. She kissed a trail starting with the corner of his mouth, down his jaw, his neck. His pulse beat against her lips as she traced his warm skin. He smelled like soap. She could taste the sharp scent of his cologne on her tongue. Picking apart his belt was easy, but she fumbled with the button on his dark wash jeans.

She couldn't bear to look him in the eye as she dropped slowly to her knees before him. Instead, she gave her full attention to the button. She had dreamed of this moment since she was sixteen, of seeing his cock for the first time, of touching it. She knew the first taste would be like a powerful drug. But never had she thought she'd struggle to get it out of his pants.

Finally, the button slipped through the hole. Gently she eased the zipper down. She leaned closer, inhaling as she rubbed her cheek against soft fabric that housed his erection. Her mouth watered in anticipation.

Growing up together, she'd seen him go from a thin, lanky boy to a well-toned lean man. He was built with long sleek muscle that cored his arms and legs and beaded tight in his abdomen. He'd always cared for his body, and his skin reflected a diet of low sugar. He'd never had a pimple, or a blemish. She'd seen him in swimming trunks, and she'd seen him in boxer briefs, but she'd never seen him naked. She wanted that now more than ever.

She grabbed the hem of his t-shirt and rose, bringing it with her. He raised his arms as they stripped him of his top. It dropped to the floor. He would have caressed her face, brought her in for his kiss, but she avoided his hands, instead dropping once more to the ground.

This time her fingers looped through the holes that his belt occupied. She dragged the material down, but it snagged on his ass. Running her fingers along his waist, she worked to ease the denim down. Soon he stood before her in his boxer briefs. Glancing up from her crouched position by his feet, she couldn't help but smile at him. His fingers clenched around the edge of the bar as she looked him over, a feast she had been waiting years to consume.

The rough hairs on his legs rubbed against her palms as she followed the smooth lines of his calves, his muscled thighs. She cupped his ass and buried her face in his crotch. Unable to resist any longer she licked the bulge through the cotton.

"Amelia," he whispered on a strangled moan. "I won't wait much longer. I want your mouth on me, now."

Silently obeying, she slipped off his underwear. They joined the pile around his ankles. His erection stood reaching out toward her from a patch of dark hair. She knew he regularly waxed his chest, but not even a *happy trail* remained. The knowledge that the women who ogled him at the gym only ever saw his naked chest, that they wouldn't ever get a glimpse of his pubic hair made her happy. This was all for her. Her treat.

Amelia licked her lips.

She took him in her hand and stroked him, familiarizing herself with his size, his girth. She watched the catch in his breath as she stroked him softly, and then grasped him harder, learning how he liked to be touched. After a few minutes of letting her play, his eyes flicked opened, the blue of his irises so intense she could see them from where she knelt.

She could see he was about to speak, to command her once again to open her mouth and take him in. She spoke instead,

"You're everything I knew you'd be."

Then she tasted him.

* * * *

He watched as she bent her head and licked him. He couldn't tear his eyes away. She traced the crown of his penis with her tongue, licked him from base to tip before opening her mouth and sucking him inside.

Cradling her head with one hand, Nick let her explore, all the while he tried not to thrust into her mouth. When she widened her lips and took him deeper, he dropped his head back and released a long moan. On a shaky laugh, he muttered, "Yes, baby, just like that."

Encouraged, she took him deeper still, testing her own limits. When his pre-cum formed at the tip, she greedily licked it away. Her insistent tugging beat at his control. She ran her hands across his thighs to cup his balls. She massaged the mass with one hand, held him firm with the other.

He was slipping faster than he wanted. If he had jerked off last night he might have stood a better chance of holding on longer tonight, but like a fool he'd waited up for her. Now, this erotic act she gifted him with would end too soon. Ah, well, he'd just have to get her to do it again later, and again, and again...

She devoured him and took him deeper until he could feel the back of her throat closing around him. His grip tightened in her hair as his hips thrust toward her.

"Oh, fuck, Amelia, I'm going to come." What she did with that information was up to her, and she didn't disappoint. She stayed with him until the very end. On a broken moan, he came. Her soft mewing sounds filled his ears as she drank him down.

His body ceased convulsing and his hold on her hair

relaxed. She pulled away, her tongue dragging over him, wiping him clean. Using the back of her hand, she cleaned her mouth and looked up in triumph, her eyes sparkling.

The pad of his thumb brushed over her lips. "That was incredible. Thank you."

"You're welcome." Her grin was mischievous.

He stepped out of the puddle of his clothing at his feet. "There is one problem though. You're wearing too many clothes."

She tapped her lip in thought. "That is a problem."

"Rascal." He hauled her to her feet and before she had a chance to argue, he hefted her up, urging her to wrap her legs around him. He was weak kneed from the blowjob she'd given him, so the couch seemed the most logical place to go. With her ass resting in his hands, he took a moment to bury his face between her boobs. God, she had a terrific rack, filling out her C-cups perfectly. She laughed and cupped his head in her hands, cradling him, encouraging him. He breathed her in, but he touched clothing where he wanted skin.

In three strides, he made it to the couch and dropped her.

"Whoa!" She bounced upward, but he didn't give her time to get coordinated. Pulling her legs apart, he settled between them, grabbed her chin and kissed her.

She tasted salty, she tasted like him. As they kissed, he worked her shirt up over her breasts. He wanted to touch her tits, but as she rocked beneath him, he realized getting her pants off was more pressing. The jeans she wore rubbed uncomfortably against his dick. He couldn't believe how hard he still was. If they kept this make out session up, he'd be ready to go again, and soon, but he wanted to be sure she was ready first. He wanted to watch her come, to feel her struggle in ecstasy.

He flipped open the two buttons and unzipped her, while she discarded her bunched up tank top. He shifted and dragged her pants off. She didn't protest when he took her thong along with them. He tossed it all away.

As he crawled back over her body, she curled up to meet him, urgently dragging his mouth to hers. When she sat up, he intended to get rid of the bra, but when he reached behind her, she stopped him. "It undoes in the front."

He merely grunted in response, and flipped the magnetic clasp apart. He shoved the fabric away. Amelia quickly threw the bra aside, her breasts jiggling with the effort. She reclined once more, her smile calling to him. He leaned over her and drew one taunt nipple into his mouth. God, she tasted good.

She cooed while he massaged one breast and tongued the other. He switched from one to the other, her body surging beneath him. He didn't understand where his sudden sense of urgency came from, but he needed to taste her, to make her come, *now.*

With his fingers, he traced the lines of her stomach. He inched lower and caressed the seam where her thigh met her body. She arched into his touch. He knew what she wanted. Lightly at first, he ran the tips of his fingers over her vulva. As if he was petting a cat, he drummed his fingers again and again over her sensitive flesh.

She wiggled and squirmed, wanting him to press his fingers inside, or touch her clitoris, but he avoided both. Her feet dragged up the backs of his legs, silently pleading, but he wanted to hear the words. He lowered his head and nipped at her belly button ring. He knew she was ticklish and he let his breath graze her sides.

"Please." Her moan was the most beautiful thing he'd ever heard. "Please, please, touch me."

He sank two fingers in deep and rubbed his thumb along her seam until he discovered her swollen clitoris. He would reward her begging, her asking. He shifted lower and used his tongue on her.

Removing his fingers, he used his thumbs to massage her body, to open her to him. He took his time licking, until she was nearly crying, her nails digging into the sofa. He thrust his tongue inside her, tasting her as she dampened for him. She was sweet and tangy.

He knew she wanted more. She needed something deep inside her. Again, he thrust his fingers in. He wiggled them around, and when she gasped, he knew he'd found that magical spot. She tried to stifle her moans as they increased in volume, but he didn't stop. He plunged his fingers deeper and with his tongue, he lavished her. She grabbed a fistful of his hair and tried to dislodge him as the pleasure became too intense, but he didn't stop. A moment later, she let go. Her passage seized around his fingers and eventually her death grip on his hair subsided.

He shook his forelock out of his eyes and wiped his mouth on the back of his hand, just as she had done. Watching her stretched out, relaxed on the couch made him want to do it all over again.

"I've got to get a condom."

"Okay." She smiled weakly.

He pressed up from the couch. That's when they heard it. The squeak of floorboards. Someone was moving upstairs. Panicked, Amelia propped her head up. "Fuck! What if someone heard us?"

"I doubt it." He held perfectly still.

The footsteps above them grew louder and closer. Someone was coming to the basement door. Amelia scrambled for her clothing.

The door opened and Gabe whispered down the steps, "Nick? Nick, are you still up?"

Nick was impressed with the speed in which Amelia dressed. He was shocked when she responded to her brother. "No, Gabe. It's me."

Nick made a move toward her, but she shushed him.

"Amelia? What are you doing down there?" Gabe's footsteps advanced, and Nick realized he was still naked. Only a thin layer of beige painted drywall separated the stairwell from the basement. For now, they were concealed, but if Gabe continued down the stairs, Nick had no idea how he'd explain his lack of clothing.

"I fell asleep. I'll be right up."

Nick grabbed her arm. If Gabe didn't wait for her, then she could stay, they didn't have to stop. Gabe squashed that thought. "Hey, since you're up do you want to see what I got Paige for Christmas?"

"Damn," Nick growled.

"I'm coming. Just give me a sec."

"I'll go grab it." They heard him walk back up the stairs.

Nick grasped her by the shoulders and spun her around. "We'll talk later, okay?"

She was eager to leave so she gave him a quick nod and promptly turned, but something stopped her. "You haven't told anyone, have you?"

He blinked. "No."

"Can we keep it that way? I don't want anyone to know."

That confused him. He wasn't in a rush to tell Gabe, or her family for that matter. The only person who would welcome the news would be Tammy Evans, Gabe and Amelia's grandmother. But why didn't Amelia want anyone to know?

They didn't have time to get into it. If Gabe came back down, they'd be busted.

"We'll talk tomorrow," he said again. He watched her walk away and wondered if she realized just how thorough that conversation was going to be.

Chapter Five

Amelia had been killing time on the internet. She'd checked the university website three times in hopes of seeing her marks. She'd window shopped online, took a quiz and discovered her animal spirit was a hummingbird. She read reviews for a few books and watched a couple of movie trailers. All in an attempt to keep her mind from thoughts of Nick.

Try as she may to enjoy this unexpected sexual experience, her subconscious kept whining at her. What were his motives? Why now? Dread continued to massage the outskirts of her mind. When would the other foot fall?

Gabe poked his head into her room. "Hey, Grandma and Grandpa just got here."

"Thanks." She closed the laptop and hopped off the bed. After a quick glimpse in the mirror, she followed in the direction Gabe had gone.

A rowdy reunion was commencing at the base of the stairs. Warm hugs were being exchanged. Her mother's parents, George and Tammy Evans, had moved several hours north after retiring, so it was rare that Gabe and Amelia enjoyed much time with their grandparents.

"Amelia!" her grandma cried with outstretched arms.

She'd been nervous about this visit. Since she was a young girl, Amelia had gotten along well with her grandmother and told her all her deepest secrets. Well, all but one. When she had hid away at school, her grandparents had been the most disappointed each Christmas that she was absent. She and her grandma still talked on the phone frequently. Grandma insisted that Christmas just wasn't right without the whole family.

Standing awkwardly on the stairs, Amelia beamed when, with enthusiasm, they spotted her.

After hugging and kissing each of her grandparents in turn, she linked arms with her grandma, who guided her away from the bustle at the door. Gabe began carrying the luggage up to the den.

"Want a beer, Dad?" Mom asked before disappearing into the kitchen, no doubt to pull out some appetizers.

"Sure," her grandpa said before following Gabe up the stairs.

"Now then—" Grandma led her over to the couch—"did you get back together with that boy? Last you told me you'd broken up, but your mother tells me he wanted you back, not that I'm surprised mind you, lovely girl like you."

Amelia smiled kindly. "No we are not getting back together. Sometimes he seems to think we should give it another go, but definitely not."

"Good, because you know what I think?"

Amelia rolled her eyes. *Not this again.*

"That young friend of Gabe's is much more suitable. You should never have given up so easily."

"Grandma, please."

"No, no! Everyone else around this place is blind, but not me. I know the truth. You belong with that boy."

Pursing her lips, Amelia avoided telling her grandma more than she ought. It was better that no one know about the developments between herself and Nick. This time when he crushed her heart, no one would pity her. No one would question her decisions.

"You should try again."

"Mom, you're not filling her head with nonsense again, are

you?" Amelia's mother came back in with a tray of veggies and dip. "I blame you for what happened three years ago," she said pointedly. "I've barely seen my daughter since."

"Pasha." Grandma waved her away. "A girl's got to take initiative. Back in my day it wasn't like it is today, but even then I went up to your grandfather and I said, *George Evans you'd better ask me to that Spring Fling or else!*"

Amelia and her mom exchanged a glance, brimming with laughter at the story they'd heard hundreds of times.

"Scoff all you want, but them boys are dense! Got to knock them over the head with a two-by-four to get anything through their thick skulls."

Amelia dipped a carrot into the ranch sauce. "I believe you, Grandma." Because in fact there was some truth to what she said. Masturbation and a porno had been Nick's two-by-four.

"Evelyn and Jacob and the kids should be here tonight. I thought they'd have already arrived, but maybe they stopped for dinner on the way," Amelia's mom informed them before asking what colour wine her grandma wanted.

Gabe flounced back into the room and plopped onto the opposing sofa. He gobbled up a few veggies before their grandpa made it to the bottom of the stairs. Gabe tossed a deck of cards on the table. "I've got to meet Paige for dinner, but I think I've got enough time for a game of euchre before I go."

By the time their grandpa had settled next to Gabe with a beer, the first hand had been dealt. After ensuring everyone had a drink, their mother settled into one of the free chairs and took sips from her wine glass between typing on her iPad.

"I'm glad you're still dating that girl," Grandma stated as she played a right bower and stole the final trick from Amelia and Gabe, foiling their attempt at two points. "She sounds like a peach. I can't wait to meet her."

"You'll like her, Grandma."

"Not as much as I liked that librarian you were dating last summer. Smart as a whip that one," Grandpa interjected.

"Samantha? We're still friends. I see her from time to time. Pass."

"We saw Chris on the way in," Grandma told them.

"Yeah, Dad's tinkering with the snow sleds. He's trying to get them ready for when everyone gets here," Gabe explained. Their younger cousins Camille, Lauren, and Anthony loved to race around on the snowmobiles.

Their grandpa turned to their mom. "How's business these days?"

"Good," she answered, "busy as ever."

They chatted on as the game played out. Soon Amelia and Gabe shot to their feet and did a silly victory dance while George declared they wouldn't go so easy on them the next time.

"What time do you have to meet Paige?" Mom asked.

"I'm going to go now," he was saying when his cell phone interrupted him. Answering the phone Gabe rounded the couch and paced, "Hey, man, what's up? Not much my grandparents just got here." He held the phone away from his mouth. "Nick says hi."

Amelia stiffened. Grandma chuckled. "Now isn't that Nicholas a sweet boy, Sally? Hi, Nicholas."

"They say hi back. What? I'm supposed to meet Paige for dinner." It was silent as Gabe listened to whatever Nick had to say. "Okay, yeah I'll be there."

"What's wrong?" Mom asked when he hung up the phone.

"Nick's car won't start. He's at work waiting for a tow. I'm going to have to go get him." He thumbed through his phone, looking for Paige's number.

"You can't make Paige wait." Their grandma idly shuffled the cards before innocently adding, "Amelia can go get him."

"Mom!" their mother all but yelled.

"Well, he shouldn't stand up that sweet young girl," Grandma insisted.

Sally shook her head, but didn't say anything more. Grandma nudged Amelia.

Trying not to jump at the chance to see Nick, Amelia finally huffed, "Fine, I'll go get Nick."

Gabe was pulling on his coat when Amelia got up. "Thanks, I'll owe you one."

Giving her mom a reassuring pat on the shoulder as she passed, Amelia muttered, "Yeah, you will."

* * * *

Daniela twirled a strand of blonde hair around her finger as she puffed out her chest, trying her best to capture Nick's attention. "So far I really like working here, everyone has been really friendly and the clients are wonderful. Maybe it's just the time of year."

As Daniela went on comparing this job to her last job, Nick kept casting glances out the window. The tow truck had just driven off with his beater. Half an hour ago when his shift had ended, the damn car wouldn't start. He'd checked over the battery and the starter but nothing he tried seemed to get the thing to start, eventually he'd called to have it towed it to a local garage.

Going back into the gym he'd run into Daniela, who stopped on her way out and decided to wait with him. She'd asked what was wrong after he got off the phone with Gabe and reluctantly he'd told her. He declined her offer to drive him back to the Fuller's house.

Nick glanced out the window once more, before checking his watch as she rambled on.

"Are you sure you don't want a ride?" Daniela touched his arm.

"No, my buddy's on his way." Nick kindly shrugged off her touch by pulling out his phone again. He sent a quick texted to Gabe. *Where are you?*

Daniela didn't hide her disappointment and pouted. A moment later, she burst into another smile. "What are your plans for Christmas?"

Nick chatted with her all the while wondering why she hadn't left the gym yet. Her shift was over. Didn't she have plans, somewhere to go rather than chatter at him like a freaking bird? He didn't understand why it took so long for his female co-workers to get that he didn't date fellow employees.

When his phone buzzed, relief rushed him. *Amelia offered to pick you up.*

A few minutes later Gabe texted again. *She's not there yet?*

Nick messaged back to assure him it probably wouldn't be long, but he wondered what the hell was taking her so long.

Finally, Amelia pulled up in her little red mustang.

"Ride's here." Nick immediately pushed away from the wall and exited the building. Daniela followed close behind, unwilling to be forgotten. Ignoring her clearly wasn't working. He needed a more direct approach.

Amelia parked the car close to the building in one of the empty spaces. Typically this time of day was busy and the parking lot would be full, but so close to the holidays people generally skipped the gym in favour of Christmas shopping or family time. It would pick up again as soon as the New Year hit.

Amelia hauled her pert little ass out of the car and scurried across the pavement to greet him. "I'm sorry I'm late."

Behind him, Daniela muttered, "I thought your buddy was picking you up."

Nick couldn't hide the triumphant smirk on his face. Amelia handed him a paper cup. "I stopped for coffee."

Nick ignored her outstretched offering and instead tilted

her chin upward before bending to press a kiss to her lips. It wasn't nearly as passionate as he would have liked, he didn't linger long, but his message to Daniela was clear. Stunned, Amelia wavered while he took the hot beverage from her.

"Thanks."

Daniela quickly sputtered, "Well, night, Nick," before high tailing it toward her car.

Amelia looked around the parking lot. "Where's your car?"

"They took it like half an hour ago."

Amelia winced. "Sorry, I thought I'd grab us a treat, but I got stuck in the drive thru for what seemed like forever."

"No problem. Shall we?" He opened the door for her to slide in before rounding the car to the passenger side. He tossed his gym bag into the back seat, and soon they were on their way. Amelia reached over to turn down the radio. Flurries bounced off the windshield as they made their way out of the parking lot and started heading away from the city.

Sexual tension hugged the air. Last night they had steered their relationship on a new course. The memories of the carnal pleasures they'd shared had him fighting boners all day. For years, his body had reacted to hers. A whiff of her soap or the innocent brush of her arm against his could send a chill down his spine. He'd never let himself think about her. She had been off limits, but now he couldn't stop fantasizing as though all the years of repressed dreams and images had snared the rational part of his brain. He felt like a randy teenager again. He no longer had control over his thoughts or his body, and he simply didn't give a fuck.

"You can turn the seat warmer on, if you want." Amelia made a right turn.

"Yeah, sure." Nick stretched out his legs and reached for the button to turn up the heat. His fingers hit hers as she attempted to accommodate him.

"I should have thought about it before and had it on for

you."

He hit the button twice and grabbed her hand before she had a chance to pull back. Linking their fingers, he pulled her hand toward his lap. He couldn't wait to get inside her.

"Um..." Her brow furrowed.

"Is this not okay?" He rubbed his thumb across her palm.

Amelia swallowed. "No, it's fine. It's great. It's just... I've been wondering about some stuff."

Nick raised her hand. "Like what?" he asked before drawing the tip of her middle finger into his mouth.

Her nostrils flared and for a moment, she took her eyes off the road. She seemed to struggle with her words before they came gushing out. "I, well, I... I wanted to know exactly what is going on between us. I don't want to presume anything. Last night was great."

"It was," he mumbled around her finger. *Tonight's going to be even better.*

"But we're not done yet, right?"

He removed her finger. How could she think that? "Fuck no." He readjusted his grip on her hand and pulled her middle finger into his mouth as deep as he could. He wrapped his tongue around it and sucked, *hard.*

Amelia's head rolled back against the headrest. She wiggled in her seat and bit her lip.

"Are you wet for me yet?"

Her hips arched upward, but she didn't answer.

"I asked you a question." Her eyes darted to his. "If I have to repeat myself you won't like the consequences."

She looked back at the road. Her cheeks turned red as she meekly whispered, "Yes."

Once they turned onto William Avenue, it would only be a few minutes before they pulled into the Fuller's driveway. He needed to get her to agree to come back downstairs again. "Tonight, when everyone's gone to bed, I want you to come downstairs. Wear that blue robe again."

She didn't respond.

"I hoped that we could talk about this. I want to take this whole BDSM thing seriously, but I think we need to discuss it a bit first. Lay down some ground rules. I don't want to end up hurting you. I need to know what you're willing to do. Like last night, I would have never thought you'd be willing to do that."

"Do what?" She frowned and pulled her hand from his in order to guide the car into the drive.

"Swallow."

"Oh." She grinned. "That."

As soon as she had the car in park, he dove across and kissed her the way he'd wanted to since she picked him up. Amelia was just as enthusiastic. Their tongues mated as they struggled to grab each other, a difficult task with all the winter layers on. For now, Nick had to be content to simply stroke her cheek, her jaw. He brought the kiss to a close and, as though searching for a distraction, Amelia grabbed her coffee and took a sip.

"Thanks for picking me up."

"No problem. Do you need a ride tomorrow?"

"Nah, I'm off. But if I can talk Gabe into a workout I'll bum a ride with him, sometime before the party. About tonight..."

"Yeah?"

"Will you come downstairs after everyone's gone to bed?"

He had no idea what she was searching for as she studied his eyes, but he found himself holding his breath as she debated her answer.

Nick smiled when she finally agreed. "Be sure to wear the blue robe. I'd hate to have to punish you again. On second thought I might like that."

Amelia laughed and slipped the door open. "We'll see."

Likewise, Nick exited the car, but couldn't stop the internal debate. Would it be better if she did as she was told, or if she deliberately disobeyed him? He was finding that he rather enjoyed the idea of dominating Amelia. He was excited to take it to the next level, his mind working in overdrive, developing all sorts of scenarios that would please them both.

He grabbed his gym bag from the back seat. His piece of crap car would need to be replaced, but he was glad he'd taken the time to go shopping before work that morning. His anticipation grew as he thought about the surprises he had in store to make this a Christmas Amelia would never forget.

As Nick approached the front door, he heard a shuffling noise near the garage. Casting a sideways glance, he noticed a red glow just outside the garage door.

Just perfect! He was so not ready to do this now.

"Go in, I'll be there in a minute."

Amelia shrugged and continued into the house.

Pasting on a cheerful grin, Nick bounded back down the steps and strode across the pathway to the garage. The shape of a man became more visible. Stepping out of the shadows the yellow light from the garage illuminated the man's outline as he took another drag from his cigarette.

"Hey, Chris." As he greeted Amelia's dad, Nick kept the fear from his voice the best he could. This was the man who had on occasion yelled at him like his own father should have. He'd chastened both Gabe and Nick several times for misdeeds, a few of them for teasing Amelia.

"Nick." The man inclined his head after exhaling a long stream of smoke.

"So..." Nick cast about for some form of topic. He gave up, deciding instead for the direct approach. He dug his hands into his pockets and tried not to look too much like the kid caught with his hand in the cookie jar. "So, how long you been out here?"

"Long enough." Chris took another puff before dropping the smoke and snuffing it out with his boot. "What are you doing with my daughter, Nick?"

Thankful for his self-control and knowing he'd only been caught kissing her, Nick merely shrugged.

"I don't want to see her get hurt."

"Neither do I. I care about her."

Chris studied him. Nick forced himself to keep his chin held high. He wouldn't be scared off by her family. Not this time.

"Amelia's a big girl. She can take care of herself."

Nick nodded his agreement.

"But you will treat her with respect." Chris crossed his thick arms over his chest. Gabe got his wide shoulders and strong frame from his father, but having worked construction all his life Chris had always seemed like something mythical to the boys. His winter coat only added to his bulk. "Understood?"

Nick nearly stepped back. Respect? He respected Amelia's wishes and desires. He respected her as a person. But when he thought back to how he'd paddled her the other night, he didn't think Chris would view it the same way. Nick had given her what she wanted, and she'd loved it.

"I'll treat your daughter the way she wants to be treated."

He saw his words being carefully weighed. Apparently his statement was suitable, for finally Chris turned to head into the garage.

As an afterthought Nick called out, "Amelia wants to keep it on the down low."

Chris's eyes narrowed. Not for one second did he believe that. "Of course *she* does."

Nick nearly bit clean through his tongue as he attempted to hold it. He badly wanted to defend himself, but feared he'd reveal too much. Instead he simply said, "Yeah, she does," before marching to the door, leaving Chris standing in the snow.

"Nicholas!" Inside, Tammy's greeting was much warmer than the chilly reception he'd just had.

Nick loved Tammy. Mostly because she was devoted to him, but he loved that she had an opinion about everything.

He toed his shoes off quickly and stuffed his coat in the closet. If he didn't get to the couch fast enough, Tammy would shuffle over to hug him. He hated seeing her wince when the winter chills weakened her joints.

"Tammy," he greeted her with a hug and gave her cheek a peck. "How are you? Can I get you a refill?" He picked up her empty wine glass. When she declined, he made the same offer to George and received a different answer. From the kitchen, he heard Tammy prattle on about starting another game of euchre.

* * * *

Tammy kept an eye on the stairs, waiting for Nicholas to reappear. He'd wanted to change from his work clothes before joining them in the living room. She was getting eager to see some great-grandbabies soon, and she wanted them to have Amelia's brown hair and Nicholas's sharp blue eyes.

She would never understand why Nicholas fought his attraction to Amelia. It seemed fairly obvious that the boy was as obsessed with her as she was with him. Well, it was obvious to her, but most of the time people just didn't pick up on the little things.

As children, Gabe and Nicholas had teased Amelia to the point of tears on multiple occasions. That was always clue number one. For years now, Tammy had caught Nicholas indulging in long looks at her granddaughter. He was sly though. His gaze never lingered long enough for Amelia to catch it, and he still buggered off with Gabe at any opportunity. But Tammy knew better. Being alone with

Amelia was simply too much temptation for the boy.

When he finally re-emerged from the basement, Tammy patted the seat next to her. "Come and sit beside me. Now that Gabe's gone, Amelia needs a new partner for euchre."

"Sure, Tammy."

He took his seat and Tammy began dealing out the cards again. He'd put on cologne when he'd changed his clothing. The effect wasn't lost on Amelia, she leaned forward in her seat.

Everyone picked up their cards.

Nicholas frowned. "Pass."

George followed suit.

"Pass," Amelia echoed, "Gabe and I won the last game. So if we lose this time I'm blaming you."

Nicholas barked out a laugh. "Fair enough."

Tammy picked up the diamond she'd flipped over, and with it, she and George won all five tricks. Nicholas dealt next.

"That wasn't a strong start, Nick," Amelia chided him before picking up her cards. She groaned at her hand, and Tammy snickered.

"Maybe Nick isn't such a great partner." George nudged Amelia and the two of them laughed at Nicholas's expense. Again Tammy and George took a point. They won the following round as well, but then Amelia dealt Nicholas an alone heart's hand.

With the score a tie, Tammy felt confident enough to point out that Nicholas had indeed come through as Amelia's partner.

"Yes, Grandma," Amelia said in hopes of appeasing her, but Tammy witnessed the look that slipped between the opposing team. *Interesting.*

As the game continued, Tammy definitely noticed that something was different between Amelia and Nicholas.

Maybe Amelia was over Nicholas as Sally had suggested, but that didn't explain the ease with which they interacted. It wasn't awkward. It wasn't tense. Something else hummed in the air.

The game was much closer than the last one. The points almost distributed equally.

"And that's game." George threw down the right bower and took the remaining trick. Tammy smiled at her husband as he collected the cards on the table.

Amelia sunk into the couch and pouted. "I blame Nick. I knew I should have left him at the gym."

With a smirk, Nicholas finished off the coffee he'd walked in with.

"Shall we play another game?" Tammy asked, wanting the opportunity to monitor Amelia and Nick's interaction for a little longer.

"Grandma! Grandpa!" three voices shouted from the doorway as their second daughter Evelyn's children pushed through the door.

Anthony, Lauren, and Camille dropped their things in the entrance and ran to meet their grandparents. Nicholas donned his coat and shoes and slipped outside to help Chris and Jacob bring in the luggage and Christmas presents from the van.

Evelyn and Sally hugged and chatted as the volume in the house increased. Tammy gathered each of her grandchildren in for a big hug before Evelyn hollered at them to put away their shoes and coats. Amelia slipped the cards back into the cardboard box and tossed out hers and Nicholas's coffee cups. She filled bowls with chips and cheese puffs.

As the adults began to commandeer the conversation once more, the children rummaged under the tree to see who had the most presents.

"Amelia!" Camille held up a thin white box, wrapped with

a purple bow. "This one is for you. It's from Nick!"

All conversations were abandoned.

Amelia stared at the little girl. The left side of Nicholas's mouth tilted upward.

"That's nice, Camille, thanks for letting me know." Casually she grabbed a handful of cheese puffs and plopped one in her mouth.

"So, Evelyn, are you ready for final exams?" Tammy turned to her daughter. Evelyn was a high school science teacher, and loved her job. It was the best way to get the attention off Amelia and Nickolas. When the discussion began a whirlwind of dialog ,Amelia mouthed a quick *thank you* her way. Tammy winked. Yes, this Christmas was sure to hold a few surprises.

Chapter Six

Running her finger along the pattern on the French style doors in the basement, Amelia toyed with the idea of knocking. Desperately she wanted to finish what she'd started with Nick, but it could only lead to disaster. After they slept together, they could never go back to being friends, if they ever really were friends. It would be so awkward when he visited the house, when he hung out with Gabe. She would be forced to see him.

At first she'd worried he knew her secret, that he could use the knowledge to hurt her, but then she realized it was just as dangerous for him to take part in a Dom/sub relationship with her. One word to her brother or her father and he'd be out on his ass, for good.

On a strangled breath, she leaned forward and rested her forehead on the doorframe.

"Are we just going to stand out here, or are you going to knock?"

She jumped. "What the hell, Nick!"

He flashed her his sexy half smile before taking a sip out of the ice water he held.

When she'd slunk down the stairs and across the main floor, she hadn't noticed anyone in the kitchen. He'd followed her back to the basement, and now he knew she'd hesitated.

Reaching around her, he pulled one of the doors open. "Do you want to stand here all night, or would you like to get started?"

Her eyes roamed over him. He was wearing black flannel

pajama bottoms and nothing else. His hair was tussled, leaving her to wonder if he'd slept while he waited for everyone else to go to bed. She'd been fixing her makeup and hair.

When she hesitated, he lowered his head skimming her cheek with the tip of his nose. She leaned into him, but he straightened. "After you."

He closed the door behind them. Motioning for her to take a seat on the bed, he took another drink before leaving the glass on the floor near the head of the bed. She tracked his movements.

"This situation isn't ideal."

Panic seized her. *He was second-guessing, too?*

"If we get caught, your dad will skin me alive, and that's if he doesn't find out about the bondage stuff."

Amelia swallowed her relief. He wasn't backing out.

"We need to establish some rules, and for now, while we're under this roof, we might have to keep a lid on the kinkier stuff. Agreed?"

Tapping her finger against her lip gave her something to focus on besides her desire to stroke his washboard abs. Taking it slow would give them a chance to see what they liked. She may have told him she was into this lifestyle, but other than the novels and dirty movies, she didn't have any exposure to what it was really like to be a sub. All she knew was that she craved it. "Agreed."

Nick was pacing back and forth across the room. Resting her hands behind her, Amelia reclined on the bed, hoping Nick would take it for an invitation.

"Let's start with safety words."

Amelia groaned. He wasn't done talking.

"Are you okay with the standard red, yellow, green?"

She rolled her shoulders, her breasts jiggling with the motion. "Yep."

"Good." He nodded. "I was checked fairly recently. I'm clean. How about you? Are you on the pill?"

"Oh." That got her mind out of the gutter and brought her back to attention. "No, I just got off it. I wasn't planning on hooking up anytime soon."

His pacing stopped, his eyes darkened. "So for now we'll stick to condoms."

For now. She clung to those words. "I'm clean though, last time I checked." Amelia settled back onto the bed. With that out of the way, surely now they could get on with the good stuff.

"When you come down here for our agreed upon time, I want you to wear this blue robe. If not, you'll be punished. If you're late, like today, you'll be punished. If you question me, you'll be punished. If you hesitate to follow a command, you'll be punished. If I ask you a question I expect a prompt and direct answer, or you'll be punished. Is that clear?"

"Yes."

Using two fingers, he tipped her chin up. "And when we're down here, when we are in play mode, you'll address me as Sir."

Amelia laughed. "You're joking, right?"

He leaned closer, his sharp scent encasing her. "This is what you wanted. What you asked me for. Isn't it?"

Amelia swallowed her pride. "Yes, Sir."

His smile grew. "Good, then let's get started. Lose the robe."

Amelia choked. He had to be joking, but when the serious expression on his face persisted, her back straightened. She hadn't been expecting to feel so on display.

They stared at each other. Neither moving. The tension building.

Part of her still wondered if this was some kind of twisted trick that would backfire on her. Was he really willing to have sex with her, to comply with her deepest desires? Her gaze travelled over him again. His dark nipples slightly protruding from his firm pecks, his belly button nearly disappearing in the artwork of his abs, the clean lines of his hipbones like a map that pointed the way to the treasure tucked away beneath the cotton.

God, he was hot. Her fingers ached to touch his tanned skin. She badly wanted to believe he wanted her as much as she wanted him.

He arched an eyebrow as she continued to hesitate. When he dropped his gaze to inspect some imagined speck of dirt beneath his fingernail, Amelia assumed he was going to call it quits on their game. Maybe he didn't have it in him after all.

Then, smooth and steady, his voice emanated through the room. "Now, Amelia."

As though in a trance, she leaned forward, peeling the robe off her shoulders to let it slither to the mattress.

Heat licked his features as he took in her naked body. She was glad in that moment that she'd forgone panties. He'd probably be mad if she'd worn more than just the robe.

"Toss it on the floor."

It was awkward to drag it out from under her, but she managed to toss it away. He came to her then, his hand slipping beneath her hair to cup her nape. Nudging her knees apart, he edged closer and pulled her into his kiss. She greedily accepted matching his enthusiasm. His mouth was warm and welcoming and suddenly it seemed too long since their last kiss.

With a will of their own, her hands rose to his drawstring, eager to see him just as nude as she. She pulled the strings free, but he stopped her before she could dip her hands in. "Not until I tell you." The words were barely out before he went back to devouring her mouth.

She licked into his mouth, her hands drawing through his

hair. Slowly he urged her to recline, his body covering hers. His erection grew as he slid it between her thighs, his hips rocking against hers. She moved with him, her body throbbing, so aware of every inch of him.

Nick tore his mouth away from hers. "Fuck! I can't slow down with you."

* * * *

His arms were shaking as he rose above her, his breath coming in pants like some sort of animal. What was happening to him?

The need to fuck her consumed his being. If he didn't slow down he'd never be able to keep up this dominance persona, and they needed it. Building up the anticipation would heighten Amelia's pleasure. She needed him to take control. His emotions were overpowering him, and if he kept up this pace, he might do something stupid, like declare himself. It was not the time for that. He needed to slow the fuck down.

Nodding to the headboard, he told her to shimmy up the bed. Her breasts jiggled as she complied.

From his crouched position at the foot of the bed, he glanced up at her, stretched out before him like a feast. A chill ran down his spine, his nerve-endings alive with pleasure at the wicked plans he had laid out for her for the next several days. He remembered the feel of her hot mouth on his cock and his balls tightened.

Lightly he took hold of her ankles and, placing feather soft kisses along the lines of her legs, made her tingle with the same awareness that held his senses captive. She shivered and quaked, her legs sprawled apart with a will of their own. From where he sat, he had an excellent view. She kept her body well maintained, her cunt bare but for the neatly trimmed triangle of curls above her mound. Her pussy lips glistened as her excitement deepened.

His fingers trailed along her smooth legs until he gripped just above her knees. Knowing the closer he got the more she'd squirm, Nick held her pinned and kissed a path up the sensitive skin of her inner thighs. Light stretch marks, barely visible, etched her skin in the places where her body had swollen in order to accommodate her sexual curves. He licked his way over her hips and nipped her belly button ring, avoiding altogether the place she wanted him to touch, to lick the most. The place she struggled to push toward him.

Rising above her once more, Nick braced himself on one arm and used his free hand to toy with her nipples. They were excited, but he wanted them primed, peaked, prepared for what he had in store.

She groaned, thrusting her pelvis against his. Wrapping her arms around his shoulders, she tugged him closer, guiding his mouth to hers. He accommodated her, their tongues at play, but when she took his tongue deep into her warm, wet mouth and sucked, he was lost.

Carefully he reached up and plucked her fingers from twirling in his hair. The motion of her kiss was drugging, and Nick did his best to keep his wits. When she finally let him up for air, he forced her hands toward the head of the bed.

With one hand, he held her pinned to the bed, with the other he searched beneath the pillow. Distracting her as best he could, Nick drove his hips against hers, rocking in a sensual rhythm. He'd hoped to relieve some of the need cursing through his veins, but with her eyes closed, Amelia arched under him driving him mad. A lifetime with this woman wouldn't be long enough to explore all the things he wanted to try with her.

Amelia didn't notice when he released her and pulled the tape he'd purchased earlier out from under the pillow, but the second she heard him rip it apart, her eyes shot open, her body stilled. Panic laced her gaze when she glanced up at him, then at the tape.

"Don't move."

"Umm..."

He hushed her. "Keep your hands together, stay just like that, or you'll be punished."

"But..." She was nervous.

"Relax." He nipped the end of her nose before whispering for her to trust him. The tape stuck to itself rather than adhering to skin and hair, so after wrapping it around her wrists, he sealed it to itself. "There."

She tested it, to no avail. He smirked.

* * * *

Straddling her thighs, Nick rose above her like some glorious dark god, looming over his human sacrifice. She gulped.

Pulling against the tape did her no good. It didn't budge an inch, her wrists remained secured.

He drummed a light caress down the sensitive skin of her arms, across her neck. His fingers played over her collarbones, tracing the hollow at the base of her throat, before he settled on her breasts, cupping each one, feeling their weight, driving her mad with need.

Leaning over her, his forelock dropped slightly over his brow. Immobile, and impatient, she was stuck, waiting for his next move, his next instruction. His cock pushed against her belly, his rough fingers stoked her nipples, his blue gaze held her soul as trapped as he held her body. Then came his soft whisper. "Mine."

She nodded slightly. "Yes."

Softly he kissed her, his lips lingering.

Pulling back, he cast another glance down her body. Reaching past her, he took the glass of water off the floor. He dipped his fingers into the iced water. Soaked, his fingertips lingered over the rim of the container, a wicked glow lighting his eyes.

Her muscles clenched in anticipation. He'd teased and tormented her as a child, so it wouldn't have surprised her one bit if he flicked water at her. Instead, he raised his hand over her, the water running to each fingertip, puddling and hovering. Mesmerized they watched as the droplets fell from him and landed in the valley between her breasts.

Amelia gasped, her nipples pulling tight with the sudden chill. With the glass still in his hand, Nick leaned down and licked the liquid from her body. The contrast of the cold water and his warm mouth sent shock waves rippling over her nerve-endings. She couldn't help the wanton way her breast lifted, each peek greedily wanting his mouth on it. He ignored them, going again to the glass for more. He repeated the action three more times until she finally begged him for more.

Throughout the day, a light stubble had accumulated over his jaw. With his five o'clock shadow, his dark eyebrows and piercing blue eyes, he was a wet dream come true. The left corner of his mouth drew upward and her vaginal walls clamped. His eyes warned of a wicked wit, constantly taking everything in, planning his next move, but whenever his lips twisted into that devious smile, that was when Amelia knew she was in trouble.

Raising the glass once more, he took a long sip. Captivated, she tracked his Adam's apple as it worked with each swallow. She fought against her restraints, dying to get her hands on his body.

Nick put the glass of water on the floor again. Still holding her lower limbs hostage between his thighs, Nick cupped her breasts. The area between them was damp from the water and his tongue. He pushed them together and rubbed his thumbs back and forth over the twin peaks.

Lowering his head, Nick drew the right one into his mouth. In shock, Amelia's back jumped off the mattress. His mouth was freezing and, when she felt the hard hunk of ice, she knew why. She squirmed beneath him, trying to escape the frozen thrill, all the while ripples of pleasure cascaded down to her clit. Each time the ice circled her nipple, her body pulsed with the need to be filled.

He released the first nipple, turning his attention to the second. Now that it was free to feel that cool air of the basement, the first one was almost painful in its arousal. As he used his tongue and the cube to play with her, he brought his hand up to tweak the first nipple. She clamped her teeth together to keep from crying out. It was hard to tell where the pain stopped and the pleasure began, all she knew was she was so attuned to his every movement, awaiting his next touch, his next lick. All the while, he held her legs captive, the only relief she could give her pussy was the little wiggling she attempted, not nearly enough to satisfy her.

When the ice had melted, she was panting.

Nick licked a trail up her neck, the temperature of his mouth changing with each inch he climbed. His mouth caressed her neck before he sucked her earlobe into his mouth. His teeth grazed it, his tongue soothed it, and his naked chest rubbed against her rigid nipples.

"How was that?" he breathed.

She moaned in bliss.

Nick pinched each of her nipples like he was tuning a radio. She jolted. "Direct answers. How was that?"

She hesitated and her nipples again paid the delicious price.

His words were hot at her ear. "I want to hear the dirty thoughts you have in that twisted little brain of yours." He enunciated each word by pulling her nipples. "*Now. How. Was. That?*"

She didn't know why but she had to provoke him.

Dragging her eyes open, she asked haughtily, "You can't tell?"

He snickered against her skin. "Wrong answer, Amelia." He stretched his arm over the side of the bed. She heard the ice clink against the side of the glass. "I've got plenty of ice left, and I think I may have missed a spot." His other hand glided down to cup her mound.

Her eyes shot wide open. No way would he think to touch her with ice down there, *would he?* She gulped, but her pride kept her from saying a word.

With his knee, he nudged her legs apart before using his damp fingers to weave a path up her thighs, leaving her skin wet and her body on fire for his touch.

As he spoke, he moved down the bed, then went fishing for another cube of ice. "When you answer my question, I'll fuck you, until then..." He sucked the cube out from between his fingers and lowered his head.

He anchored her legs to the bed with his arms, with his thumbs he parted her pussy lips, exposing her clit. When he pressed the ice against her, she cried out, struggling in his grasp.

Pushing the cube around in his mouth, he glanced up at her. "You have to be quiet or you'll get us both in trouble."

Nick dipped again and ran his tongue over her exposed flesh. It was cold, but his lavish attention was so worth it. He licked her again and again, sometimes using the cube, other times he moved his thumb to give her clitoris the pressure it desired, but it still wasn't enough.

Parts of her would begin to go numb, then his delicious tongue or his talented fingers would endeavour to warm her back up. The ice dulled her ability to feel, making his touch, his strokes all the more prominent.

In an attempt to keep quiet, she locked her fingers together, clenching her hands. Squirming, she tried to get to that magical point, but the light touches kept her too far away from the orgasm she craved. If he would just slip his fingers inside her maybe she could get there, but he deliberately skirted her entrance. He wanted her submission, but the words clung inside her mouth.

His hand left her. When she heard him again sloshing in the glass, she opened her eyes. He was staring at her. Longing laced his eyes, his smile was gone. He was concerned for her. "You okay so far?"

Undulating beneath him, she whispered, "Yes."

His lips curved up. "I need a colour answer."

She frowned then realized he was keeping the game alive. "Oh, green. *Very, very* green."

He chuckled. Popping in another ice cube, Nick began his descent again, but Amelia protested. "Wait!"

His eyebrow rose, but all she could manage was to bite her lip. She refused to beg for him, she had to keep some sense of pride, but my god she was teetering on the edge. Pleading with her eyes, she arched backward, pushing her tits toward him. Surely he'd give in.

He shook his head at her. He plucked out a second ice cube, his eyes casing his target. Placing the cold mass on her tummy, he rested it against her belly button ring. Her body instinctively sunk away from it, but there was no escape.

Crawling over her he lowered his mouth to hers, she greedily accepted his tongue, the hunk of ice moving back and forth between their mouths. She wasn't nearly ready for him to pull away. "Just answer the question and I'll fuck you so hard you won't be able to see straight."

She whimpered when he moved down the bed. "How is it, Amelia?"

Using his index finger, he circled the ice on her stomach numbing a little more of her abs with each ring he drew. Slowly melting, it was accumulating a puddle beneath it.

"Don't let this fall." He instructed before settling once more between her thighs.

Twice he licked over her sensitive clit before he opened her and jabbed his tongue inside. If she bucked, the ice would fall. Her body screamed at her to answer his damn question, but her brain stubbornly refused.

He pushed the ice cube against her opening, his tongue tracing around and around it. He used his fingers on that glorious bundle of nerves, his free hand snaking up to grab a boob. Her body's juices mixed with the melted water and ran down her crack, soaking the bedspread, turning her on even more.

Thrashing her head on the pillow, her teeth clenched, her toes curled, she finally gave in. "It's so fucking hot. I'm on fire. Please. I can't take anymore."

* * * *

Music to his ears. Her hot little pussy combined with the warmth of his mouth caused the ice to dissolve too quickly. If she hadn't given in, he'd soon need to go for another cube.

His dick twitched, reminding him how badly he needed to bury it deep inside Amelia's tight body. Being Amelia's Dom would require patience, but he hadn't realized how her reluctance to obey would cause him suffering. She held onto her dignity far too long. But he supposed that's what made it so much fun, and so damn hot.

She was waiting for his response. The need in her eyes engulfed him. He'd never wanted a woman as badly as he wanted Amelia.

He chewed the remaining ice in his mouth. In what he assumed was relief, her body went limp, her head hitting the pillow.

Nick moved up the bed, dragging the ice from her stomach

upward. He used it to outline the circumference of her breasts, helping it to melt. Tracing the column of her throat, he ended by smoothing the small bit across her lips. When she parted them, he dropped the ice into her mouth, following it in with his own tongue.

Soon the chill that had taken hold of his tongue eased as their kiss continued and deepened. He peeled the tape off, bringing her hands down to grab his cock. Amelia purred into his mouth as she eagerly accepted the task of preparing him.

When the kiss came to a close, Nick reached above their heads to the shelving unit at the head of the bed to retrieve the condom he'd put there. Enjoying her soft touch, he passed her the condom. "Here."

Curling upward, she peppered his chest with light kisses as she rolled the condom into place.

Her hand on his dick faltered when he reached down to caress her. Using two fingers, he circled her entrance, warming her body up after his frosty foreplay. A crease formed between her brows as she attempted to focus on stroking him.

Looking at her with rosy cheeks, pleasure encasing her features, he couldn't help but feel charmed.

She moistened his fingertips. Applying her body's natural lubrication, he slickened her folds, teased her swollen clit and finally dove first one, then two fingers inside her. Groaning her appreciation, she gently rode his hand while he pushed deep and pulled out only to push in deeper still.

"Are you ready for me?" he whispered.

"God, yes."

"Lay back."

Reclining, she waited for him to come to her. Positioning himself, he pressed in the first few inches, ensuring he had the right spot, the right angle. When he felt her body's wet welcome, he nearly groaned in relief. He lowered himself onto his forearms and used his thumbs to stroke her cheeks. Softly, he commanded, "Look at me."

Her lashes swept open. As he pushed deeper, inch by inch she kept his gaze. Her lips parted on a delicious inhale, pushing her breast flatter against his chest. Slowly he took her, the pleasure almost agony at their current pace, but Nick wanted to feel it all as he occupied her.

In her to the hilt, he kissed her to keep from uttering the feelings that were overwhelming him. The last thing he wanted to do was scare her off. He was sure a part of her probably still hated him for his rejection years ago.

Ending the kiss, he laid his forehead on hers and began withdrawing. His movements slow, he pulled all the way out and gradually pushed back in. Keeping up the steady rhythm, he began making love to her, their tempo increasing.

When she lifted and wrapped her legs around him, her ankles linked behind his back, she managed to take him deeper still. With a growl, he lost control, pumping into her. He reared back, holding her hips in place, his thrusts becoming more aggressive.

Amelia reached above her and pushed against the shelving, trying to impale herself deeper on his cock with each of his assaults.

He brought his thumb to rest on her clit. Their gazes found each other again, deepening their connection. With each stroke on her clitoris, her body contracted around him, forcing him closer and closer to release.

Her moans were escalating.

Nick sank toward her, his mouth claiming hers in an effort to stifle her cries. His hips ground into her, his balls hit against her ass with each lunge. She wrapped her arms around his shoulders, pulling him closer. Her vagina convulsed, squeezed him.

He pulled back and, in the cockiest voice he could muster,

whispered, "That's right, come for me."

She did. Her body bucked, her sex milking an orgasm from him. He held her hips still, burying himself deep inside, his cum spirting into the condom.

By degrees their ragged panting slowed, their bodies relaxed. Pulling out, he fell beside her. She glanced over at him, but now that they'd finished, she seemed a little uneasy, as though she thought he was going to kick her out.

Half laughing, he let out a huff of air and reached for her. "Come here."

Resting with her snuggled against him, her back stretched all along his front, he knew he'd have to get up in a minute to dispose of the condom, but for now he just wanted to hold her.

"Thanks," she mumbled, shy after their intimacy.

They laid like that for a while, just content to be with one another. Finally he raised his head, kissed the tender spot where her neck met her shoulder. "I forgot one of the rules."

She glanced over. "What?"

"For however long we're involved we'll be exclusive. I don't want any man touching you. And the same goes for me, I won't be with anyone else. You're mine and mine alone." He lightly bit her shoulder before rolling away to remove the condom. Leaving the bed, he gave her behind a playful swat. "Agreed?"

Amelia eyed him warily for a long moment. He'd thought exclusivity would have been important to her. It was certainly important to him, but as she studied him, he found himself second-guessing what she really wanted. He would have given anything to know what was going through her mind in that moment.

Finally, with a laugh, she shook her head. "Agreed."

Chapter Seven

With an hour and a half to get ready before the party, Amelia stepped out of her shower. At quarter to six, the taxi would be coming to pick her, Gabe and Nick up to take them to the party. She rubbed her long hair with the towel before draping the towel over the top of the glass shower. Taking up her comb, she ran it through her tresses, pulling out any tangles. She applied moisturizer to her face and body before entering her bedroom through the adjoining door. With the curtains pulled shut, she had no qualms about letting the cool air dry any lingering dampness from her shower. However, the little black gift bag on her bed gave her pause.

It wasn't a terribly large bag. Black looped handles hung at it sides, and bright green tissue paper stuck out the top. It rested near her pillow. A green sticky note was plastered to the side of it.

Wear this tonight.

-Nick

She hadn't locked her bedroom door or the door to her washroom when she'd gone to shower. At some point, he had snuck into her space, yet again, to plant this little present here. She suddenly wondered if he'd watched her while she was in the shower. Thank god she hadn't been singing to herself in there.

His invasion of her privacy should have left her feeling violated, but it had the opposite effect. She felt almost treasured. She hoped he'd taken the time to look in on her, to watch her while she cleaned her naked body.

Giddy, her heart pounding, she fingered the tissue paper before pulling it out of the bag. A twinge of guilt knotted in her stomach. Her little cousin Camille had already pointed out a gift to her from Nick beneath the tree. She hadn't gotten him anything for Christmas, and now he'd left her a second gift.

Whatever it was, he had something in mind for tonight, some sort of play, she thought, knowing full well that this gift wasn't something to be opened in front of other people. He enjoyed playing with her. A smile crept to her face. *Her Dom.*

Reaching into the bag, she pulled out a white box with lavender writing on it. It was a remote control panty vibrator. *Oh yes,* Nick had plans for tonight.

She inspected the toy, pulling it out of the box. Glancing over the package, she skimmed the box for the basics of the toy. Insert the light blue vibrator into the liner of a favourite pair of panties, simple enough. She peeked inside again, and not bothering with the instructional manual, she noticed that the only thing missing from the box was the remote. But Amelia knew exactly where that was.

From the moment she'd dumped Cody, she'd dreaded the idea of attending the annual Christmas party alone. After the mistletoe mishap, everyone had pitied her. Kissing him under the mistletoe hadn't gone the way she'd planned.

All their friends had viewed her as the victim, hell the whole town had. Her family had thought she was to blame, that she should have known better. Well, all but her grandmother, whose misguided advice was directly linked to Amelia's destructive decision. But now, with Nick's present, she planned to spend the evening thoroughly distracted.

Thrusting the memories away, she continued to ready herself for the party. Makeup, hair styling, plucking and primping all in preparation for a good time. She picked out a red thong to match her dress, and adjusted the vibrator inside the liner. It was discreet, just as the box claimed.

Her phone buzzed. Another text message from Cody. *I've got to see you. Tonight.*

Amelia tucked the phone into her small clutch purse before donning the new dress she'd bought for tonight. She ran her hand over the sequins. It was a bandage fit red halter dress, and as she added the silver platform pumps, she couldn't help but notice the length they added to her legs. She gave herself a once over in the mirror. Pleased, she couldn't wait to see the look on Nick's face when he saw her.

A knock sounded at her door. "Get a move on slow poke," her brother's voice came barreling through, "cab's here."

Not knowing where the night would take her, Amelia drew one shaky breath and hauled it out the door.

* * * *

Waiting at the front door with Paige, Nick rocked back and forth on his heels. He hadn't the haziest idea what to say to a preacher's daughter. Paige looked up at him through innocent eyes as they both cast about for some topic. Luckily, the awkward silence was broken as Gabe flounced down the stairs.

"Here she comes." Gabe, forever rushing, went to slip on his shoes.

"I'm not running late this time. The cab is just early."

At the sound of her voice, Nick glanced up, and his mouth literally watered. She descended the stairs with elegance and grace, her hand gliding along the metal railing, a silver purse dangling from her wrist. He'd never really noticed how long her legs were, but sleek and toned they carried her down the stairs, and with each step, her dress rode a little higher on her thighs. Long brown hair spilled over her shoulders, ending right where her nipples hid behind the red material. Her lips were bright and cherry, reflecting her choice of dress, her eyes were smoky as they caught and held his gaze.

He had to stop himself from going to the base of the stairs and kissing her senseless. He no longer had any interest in the Fuller's Christmas party, instead he wanted to march her back up the stairs and fuck her over and over again.

When she reached the last step, she tossed her long hair and gave her dress a small tug to put it back into place. His gaze stopped on her cleavage, her breasts pushed up and on display, begging to be touched.

"Wow." He couldn't stop the syllables from escaping his mouth.

He was rewarded with a slap to the back of his head. "Hey! Keep your eyes to yourself, that's my sister."

Nick smirked. Amelia's eyes lit with laughter, but she did her best to ignore the two of them. "I swear I'm not late, you, Gabe, are just obsessed with punctuality."

Gabe checked his watch. "To a fault. Now let's go, let's go. It's our parent's party and we're going to be late."

Amelia rolled her eyes as Gabe darted out the door with Paige, no doubt to help assist her into the cab. Nick took Amelia's black dress coat from her when she pulled it out of the closet. He held it out for her, and as she slipped into it, he let his fingers graze the nape of her neck. "You look incredible."

"Thanks. You don't look half bad yourself," she said, casting an eye over him.

"We'd better go before Gabe has a fit." *Or before I ravish you in the front hall,* he thought.

She turned out the lights, set the alarm, and pulled the door shut behind them. On the front porch, his breath fogged in the chilly air. "Did you get my present?"

Locking the door, she glanced up at him. "Yes."

"You're wearing it?"

Despite the cold, colour flooded her cheeks. "Yes."

"Good girl."

"I couldn't help but notice," she stated as they walked toward the waiting cab, "that part of it was missing."

"Don't you worry about that." He tapped the pocket of his black dress pants.

With Paige tucked away in the front passenger seat of the four door sedan, Nick held the back door for Amelia to slide in beside her brother before he climbed into the vehicle. When he'd called for the cab, he hadn't realized that Paige would be joining them for the short ride to the manor house. It was squishy in the back seat, but he didn't mind being pressed up against Amelia.

Soon the cab was underway.

"So what kind of car are you going to get?"

Nick glanced past Amelia to Gabe. "Not sure. I wasn't expecting this one to crap out on me just yet. I was hoping to make it through the winter."

Shifting his weight, he reached into his pocket. Beside him, Amelia tensed.

"Jumpy much?" he whispered as he withdrew his cell phone from his pocket. He flipped through a few pictures and passed the phone to Gabe. "I'm thinking about calling the guy about this one."

Gabe considered it. "Yeah, it looks okay, but why don't you think about getting a new car? You're always driving beaters, but god knows you can afford to drive something a little nicer."

The cab rolled down the road as they rambled on about the various cars and the benefits and flaws of buying a new vehicle.

The taxi ride to the manor house wasn't long. Nick and Gabe chatted about cars, while Amelia asked what Gabe and Paige had planned for the holidays. Amelia hadn't been home much in the past three years. The holidays were always busy. So far, her time with her family had been limited. Nick felt guilty for monopolizing her, but he couldn't seem to help himself. He'd missed her, too.

When they arrived at the manor, Gabe paid the cabbie before they all scrambled out of the car. The party was invite only. A line was already beginning to form at the front door. People shivered as the winter wind attempted to cut through their dress coats.

Two men worked the front door, checking to ensure those who entered were on the list, but they waved the Fullers and their guests in. Just inside the door, a pair of off-duty cops checked IDs and stamped those of age.

"I'm going to check and see if Mom needs any last minute help."

"Amelia," Paige said, "can I come, too? I'd like to help if that's okay."

Amelia disappeared down the main corridor with the preacher's daughter in tow. Nick was pretty sure Paige had an ulterior motive for offering her help.

"I don't think Paige likes me very much." Nick had a feeling she was ducking away on his account.

Gabe debated over his answer, leading Nick to assume his assumptions about the preacher's daughter were right. There was more to Paige than met the eye, something Gabe knew about, but wasn't willing to share. "Sure she likes you. What woman doesn't?" he said finally. "Not many people have arrived yet. She's probably just killing time before her friends show up."

Nick shrugged it off.

Soon the party began in earnest. The younger crowd began filing onto the dance floor, the bar staff started to pick up their pace as lines began forming. At eight o'clock, the dinner buffet would be served, but with more than an hour to go guests had plenty of time to mingle and drink before food had the opportunity to slow the effects of the alcohol.

Like a wild predator, Nick maintained a constant awareness of Amelia. She wasn't always in the same room as him, but he knew where she was at all times. When a door opened, the smell of her perfume carried toward him. Over the beat of the music and the drone of multiple conversations, he could always hear the purr of her laugh. Above all, the sexual undercurrent that roared between them was like an instinctual tracking beacon.

A few times they made eye contact as she completed a task for her mother, or when she was greeting her friends near the front door. Each time he sensed her nearness, he would catch her staring at him. She wanted to keep their relationship hidden, but her desire for him was obvious. She wasn't masking her feelings. If she wasn't careful, soon everyone would know.

Then again, those who knew their story would merely chalk it up to her idolization of him. To onlookers she was setting herself up once more for a huge fall. Or maybe they thought she was reliving that night three years ago. But Nick knew the truth.

Twice he'd almost turned on the vibrator. Each time she looked at him, she was tense, waiting for him to begin the sexual torment. She would love it and she would hate it. The vibrations through her body would be glorious. Having to hide it would be like torture.

He'd sprung for the newer model, drawn in by its online features. He liked the option of being able to use the remote, or his cell phone. He hadn't bothered to bring the remote. He could use the pre-set patterns or create his own using his cell. He could make changes whenever he liked and wouldn't have to continually hold down a button. Wireless meant he had unlimited range and could touch her from anywhere, at any time.

Currently he resisted the urge to turn it on. The moment wasn't right yet. The anticipation was half the fun.

Kevin and Ed showed up late, as always. The four of them had been friends through high school. They still attended social events, got together for drinks every few weeks, played poker once a month.

Since high school, Kevin had put on a little weight around the middle. He worked at the same retail job he'd held through school, but now he ran his department. He was a lifer. He could never keep a relationship long, though not for lack of trying. Kevin had heart and tried too hard to make each woman he dated into *the one.*

Ed had been one of the few black kids that attended their high school. As the town grew and developed, so did its diversity. Now there were two local high schools and the racial diversity had expanded to include more than the Caucasian population, a few African-Americans and the handful of Korean exchange students. The growth of the town was one of the reasons Sally and Chris Fuller's businesses had blossomed so well.

Ed had been popular in school. He and Nick had been the star athletes on the basketball team. They were both tall and lean with an abundance of agility. Kevin and Gabe, with their bulky frames had favoured the football team. Like Gabe and Nick, Ed enjoyed keeping in shape and regularly joined them at the gym. After high school, Ed had joined the forces to help cover the cost of post-secondary education. He'd spent several months overseas. Although he didn't like to talk about his time in the army, and the guys never pushed him for details, it was clear he wasn't as easy-going as he had been before signing up.

"Hey!" Kevin saluted them with a beer. Of course they'd hit the bar before searching for Nick and Gabe, and by the smell of Kevin's breath, it wasn't his first one of the night.

They shook hands and fell into a natural conversation as they sipped their various beverages. Nick told them his car had kicked the bucket. They all jumped in with suggestions of what he should buy next. Ed had a buddy from the service who was selling his car, and suggested Nick should contact him. Nick took down his name and number, while Gabe tried again to convince him to buy something newer, something with a warranty.

When Paige strutted by, Gabe introduced her to Kevin and Ed. It'd been less than a year since she'd moved to town. She and Gabe hadn't been dating very long. Ed asked how they met, but Gabe dodged the question. Shortly after Paige left with her friends, Kevin wondered how long they'd been dating.

Vaguely Gabe had replied, "You know. Not that long."

Gabe wasn't supplying details, which made Nick wonder. The Fuller's attendance at church was scattered at best. It'd been years since they'd been to a service. Where *had* Gabe met a preacher's daughter?

Nick was pulled out of his musing when Ed said, "Hey, you know who's in town for the holidays?"

"Oh yeah," Kevin took a swig from his beer before making a thrusting action with his hips, "whenever she's in town she always hits me up for a little boom-shack-a-lacka."

Gabe's head hit the wall with a resounding *thunk.* Ed shoved Kevin, nearly knocking him over and laughed. "That's right, Brooke is in town."

Nick smiled at the way Gabe's back teeth ground together. Gabe glared back at him, challenging him to say even one word. Personally, he'd never understood why Brooke Holter got under Gabe's skin the way she did.

Luckily, Gabe was saved from further conversation when Sally Fuller appeared on stage. Nick pushed away from the wall and started forward. "Come on." He ushered his friends closer to the stage. The moment was almost here, and Nick wanted to be sure he had a good view.

At eight o'clock sharp, the buffet was announced. Like every year, the DJ stopped prior to the food service, and Sally took the wireless microphone from him. It took a minute or two for the crowd to quiet down, but soon more ears were tuned into her than not.

"Once again we'd like to thank you all for coming. It means so much to be surrounded by family and friends at this time of year. Fuller Homes and Construction is happy to welcome each of you to this year's festivities. Like in previous years, all the funds raised tonight will be going directly to *Create a Christmas Wish* to help families in the area enjoy a happy and fulfilling Christmas..." Sally then launched into a brief description of what the charity did and how many families go without through the holidays. She thanked the catering staff, the security team, and the DJ before reminding everyone not to drive if they'd been drinking, and that taxi services would be available for those who needed a safe option to get home. "Finally, I'd like to invite everyone to fill a plate just as soon as we say a quick prayer for the meal. It'd like to invite my daughter Amelia up to say the blessing." She swiftly searched the crowd for her daughter.

Smiling to people here and there, Amelia made her way to the little stage where the DJ stand was.

"Over the last few years Amelia has been away at school. She used to say grace for us every year. Well we're quite happy she's back now." Somewhere in the crowd came a loud shout of agreement, which was followed by a round of laughter. Sally handed the microphone over. "Will you do the honours?"

Cheerfully Amelia took the microphone and bowed her head.

With the application open on the screen, Nick fingered his cell phone.

Chapter Eight

The atmosphere in the room changed as Amelia prepared for the prayer. Most people bowed their heads along with her. In the corner of the room, someone coughed, interrupting the brief hush that had fallen over the crowd.

"O Lord, we thank you for the gifts of your bounty which we will enjoy this night."

Her panties started to vibrate, her thighs instinctively tightened at the sudden jolt of pleasure. Her head snapped up so she could search for Nick in the crowd. She could feel his gaze boldly tracing over her body. Her face heated.

She swallowed hard, but forced herself to continue. "As you have provided for us in the past, so may you sustain us throughout our lives."

She had said the prayer countless times at their family dinner table, and many times in this very room. The words were familiar, but as she waited for the next jolt of pleasure to overtake her, she found herself reaching into the corners of her mind to find the next words. "While we enjoy your gifts, may we never forget the needy and those in want—"

The vibrator buzzed again against her flesh, halting her words. She gripped the microphone harder as she fought the wave that rode her. Her mother elbowed her.

"We thank you for bringing us together on this snowy night. Amen." She tumbled the final words out as quickly as possible.

"Amen," the crowd murmured after her.

A moment later, the DJ started the next song and guests

began mingling, dancing, or heading toward the buffet.

Her mother took the microphone and clipped it off. "Thanks, honey," she whispered before giving her an affectionate kiss on the forehead.

"No problem," she lied before scampering off to find Nick in the crowd.

How humiliating. She could still feel the colour stinging her cheeks. She hunted through the moving throng of people, but couldn't find him. He seemed to know where she was though, for every few minutes the vibrator pulsed against her. Each time she stopped, her breath caught in her throat. She wished like hell she'd tested the vibrators potency before boldly sticking it in her underwear, but then she remembered he hadn't given her any such opportunity.

Her search ended when Amy and Geneva found her.

"Hey, great job up there!" Amy congratulated her

"Yeah," Geneva's attention was elsewhere, "let's go get some food."

Amelia didn't fancy the idea of eating. Not when her pussy was suddenly on fire. It was such a public arena. She needed to be able to move. "No. The line will be huge, let's dance a bit first. Let the eager ones get through the line."

Geneva groaned, but finally gave in.

"Brent should be back with our drinks any minute," Amy explained. "We left him in line with Lynn and Kenny."

Fighting the sensations that were taking over her body, Amelia grabbed her friends by the wrist and started dragging them toward the dance floor.

"Okay, okay." Geneva laughed. "Don't you want a drink first?"

"Oooh, good idea!" Booze would definitely help her problem, but rather than wait in line at the bar Amelia grabbed her friends by the wrists and started she grabbed a wine glass from a passing waiter and rapidly downed a few gulps. Her friends exchanged a glance at her odd behaviour. She challenged them. "What?"

"Nothing," they answered in unison.

"Good then let's go." She urged them once more toward the floor. About to step foot onto the oak hardwood tile she caught sight of Nick. He was leaning in the hallway talking with her brother, Ed Moore and Kevin Keys, and a few of their buddies from high school.

He must have checked his suit jacket along with his dress coat, he stood in his white dress shirt and dark blue tie. Sleeves rolled up around his muscular forearms, his hands disappeared into his pants pockets as he leaned his shoulder against the wall.

She heard him laugh at something Ed said and wondered if he even knew where she was. Perhaps he was just pressing the button in his pocket at random. Gabe clapped Ed on the back for whatever joke he had told, but Nick's gaze swung over to hers.

Caught staring at him, she barely dared to breathe. For half a heartbeat, she thought of going over to him, but realized it would be too suspicious if she suddenly abandoned her friends after coercing them into dancing. With a complacent smirk, Nick lifted one hand from his pocket to grace her with a half wave.

Struggling, she didn't respond, instead carrying on with her friends. A second later, her panties buzzed.

Amelia made a point of not looking in Nick's direction. She focused all her attention on her girlfriends. Geneva was always good at loosening the rest of them up. Lynn hated dancing. She and her boyfriend stood on the outskirts of their circle, close enough to nod along, but far enough that Geneva rarely dragged them into the middle.

Each year the same DJ worked the party. He read the crowd and switched up the music to keep everyone happy.

The night started out with the hit lists, before rolling out some country and rock. A few songs with a slower tempo would be sprinkled in later in the evening.

Dancing had always been a joy for Amelia. She refused to get caught up in appearances, and instead followed the music. The dance floor was the one place she and Geneva always got along. Now, more than ever, Amelia felt empowered. She'd been going to the club with her college mates every week or so, and occasionally Cody had liked to visit clubs with a Latin flare.

As the food line dispersed, the dance floor became even more crowded. At one point Lynn convinced them to break for food. While the rest of her friends filled their plates with the delicious buffet, Amelia stuck to an assortment of cold finger foods, mostly cheeses and sliced meat. Enough to sustain her, but not enough to detain her from the dance floor for long. Lynn and Kenny directed their group to some empty chairs, but Amelia didn't linger. Within fifteen minutes, she discarded her plate and begged her friends to join her on the dance floor again.

"What's with you tonight?" Amy wondered after nibbling on a dessert Brent offered her.

"Nothing is *with me* it's just been a long time since we got to party like this. All of us together. If we sit around we'll waste it. Come on!"

Beside Amy, Brent chuckled and whispered something in his girlfriend's ear. Amelia frowned, but Amy shook her head. "No she hasn't had that much."

Dropping her head, backward Amelia suppressed a groan. Everyone thought she was acting weird, and it was all Nick's fault. *Again.* "Look, I'm going to find some people to dance with. There's got to be someone fun around here. But if you aren't back out there in ten minutes I'm going to drag you out there." Amelia paused for effect, looking each of them in the eye.

Disappearing into the crowd, Amelia shifted and bumped her way through the people. She spotted a few women she'd worked with in high school bobbing along to a *Taylor Swift* song. When they waved, she headed their way, but her mother intercepted her, requiring her help on a few various tasks, and demanding that Amelia meet and greet with a few of her co-workers and clients.

Twenty minutes later, after she'd seen her grandparents off in a cab, she found her father on the patio having a smoke with Kevin and Ed.

"Hey, Dad, guys." Amelia nodded at Gabe's friends before delivering a message to her father. "Mom's looking for you."

"Okay. I'll go find her in a minute." Lacking haste, her dad took another puff on his cigarette and resumed leaning against the wall.

Amelia turned to head back inside, but changed her mind. The winter breeze brushed across her skin. Snow was falling lightly from the sky, adding to the scattered dusting that was on the ground. The cobblestone patio was illuminated by twinkling white Christmas lights draped around the windows and the cedar bushes.

She took the opportunity to pull her hair back from her neck and let the cool air bring her fevered flesh some relief. It was then that she noticed the absence of shock waves in her panties. She hadn't felt vibrations since she'd eaten. Instantly she wondered what Nick was doing that was keeping him so preoccupied. Then she cursed herself for caring.

"By the way Grandma and Grandpa went back home."

"It's not that late, is it?" Her dad checked his watch and shrugged. It was almost eleven.

Someone pinched her sides from behind. She squealed and instinctively shot her elbow back at her intruder. Her attack narrowly missed Gabe's stomach. Laughing, he joined their group, Nick with him, his fingers gliding over the surface of his phone. He barely glanced up in greeting.

Grinding her back teeth, Amelia fought the jealousy that was creeping into her awareness. Really she didn't care who he was texting on his phone, or whatever it was he was doing.

"Amelia, we grabbed you another drink." Amy and Brent suddenly appeared beside her. "Did you want to go dance now?"

Looking in Nick's direction again, Amelia decided she'd better go before anyone suspected something. As far as everyone knew, he'd jilted her years ago, and from the way, he was acting now it seemed the status quo hadn't changed.

She took the offered drink and had a sip before answering with a smile. "Yeah, sure."

"Hold up," Brent said, his gaze caught on Amelia's dad. "Chris, I just wanted to thank you again for all the help you've given us."

Amy's attention was promptly stolen. She launched into a discussion with the men about the construction that was going on. Amelia quietly sipped her drink. Listening a little more intently whenever they brought up the house that was being built for Nick. When she was at school, her mom had mentioned something one evening during their weekly phone calls about Nick purchasing a new build from Fuller Homes and Construction. Gabe and Nick had been lending the construction crew a hand whenever they had free time. It would be ready in the spring.

After graduating a few years ago, Gabe had started working for their dad, and since then his architecture degree had been put to use. Able to use his expertise, and their father's contacts, Gabe had become an overnight success in the construction world. He and Nick had taken business and management courses at night and now Gabe was successfully running his own business. He paid their parents rent money, but it was beyond Amelia why he still lived at home. If she had his kind of money and background, she would have built herself a fabulous house by now.

Since returning from overseas, Ed also worked for their father. He'd started framing but quickly moved onto roofing and was currently learning how to install the plumbing. Gabe had told her that Ed was making plans to apprentice for an electrician next. Ed was obviously a fast learner, who liked to be kept busy.

Amy's knowledge of the construction was coming to a close. Amelia could feel her friend's interest beginning to wan. Kevin leaned over and whispered something to Nick. He looked up from his phone and laughed.

The vibrator started again.

Her fingers tightened on the glass she held. The vibrator rippled against her swollen flesh. With her panties already soaked, they clung to her with each movement she made. She pinched the bridge of her nose and fought the sexual thrill. The speed increased. Amelia lowered her hand and raised her drink, praying the alcohol would take the edge off.

That's when it hit her that Nick's hands weren't in his pockets. *Who was controlling the vibrator? Had he given it to someone else?*

Amelia nearly choked. She couldn't call him out in front of all these people, and she couldn't ask to speak to him privately, less someone figure it all out. So she took out her cell phone and texted the jackass.

Amelia: *Where's the remote? Who's got it?*

Across the group, Nick glanced down at his phone. His brows pinched together. Confusion etched his features as he looked up at her.

Nick: *No one.*

Amelia: *This thing just turned on by itself. Is it defective?*

The left corner of Nick's lips lifted. A second later Amelia's phone vibrated in her hand.

Nick: *Nope. It's a fairly upgraded toy. It's got an app. I didn't bring the remote.*

Subtly Nick wiggled his phone, his lips pursed to keep from laughing.

Nick: *I can control it from my phone. See?*

His fingers worked over the phone. The clitoral stimulation stopped, there was a brief pause before it suddenly gave off staccato like flicks of pleasure against her.

Her third orgasm of the evening shattered her composure. Fortunately, it was smaller than the others that had overtaken her, but still an uncomfortable surge of wetness soaked into her panties. Amelia reached out to grab Amy's arm, her fingers digging into Amy's skin.

"Ow!" Amy rubbed her arm. "What's the matter with—" noticing Amelia's eyes locked on Nick, Amy turned and rushed her friend away from the group. "Let's go dance."

When they were a safe distance away, Amy slowed. "Serious, what's the matter with you tonight?"

"Nothing."

"Don't give me that crap. Something is going on with you and Nick. What's wrong? What's he done this time?"

Deciding she needed to level with her friend, she leaned in close to confide, "I'm wearing a panty vibrator."

Amy stepped back and laughed. "That's hilarious."

Amelia glared. "It's not funny."

"Does it work?"

"Too well."

Amy laughed all over again. "Nick's got the remote?"

Not wanting to get into it any further, Amelia just nodded and urged Amy to keep moving.

"I can't believe those things actually work."

Amelia slanted her a look. "It's beyond ridiculous. Let's go. I need to move. And not a word!"

Trotting after her, Amy couldn't resist needling her a bit. "I guess he's really staking a claim."

Amelia didn't bother to answer. She practically ran the last few feet to the dance floor, the attention in her panties alternated between various patterns and speeds. It wasn't long after they began dancing that Brent joined them again. Her father came back inside, too, no doubt looking for her mother, or perhaps looking for ways to avoid whatever job she had for him to do. Fifteen minutes later, she spotted Gabe and Nick crossing the hallway. With plates of food, Kevin and Ed soon joined them.

Trying to lose herself in the music, Amelia let her mind wander. She speculated on what sorts of things Nick had in store for her when they got home. She couldn't wait for him to touch her. Her body ached for him. It wasn't just that her cunt was on fire. Each time she received a jolt from the toy, her nipples beaded tight. Her skin felt irritated. Her mouth watered for even a taste of Nick's stunning body. Her mind grew clouded with that line of thinking, so much so that at first she didn't notice the familiar blond-haired man walking through the crowd.

Cody.

She might not have seen him if the masses hadn't parted at the right moment. Eagerly, he searched the crowd, slowly making his way toward her.

Picking Cody had been a deliberate choice. Ultimately, she'd gone for the complete opposite of Nick. She'd picked someone younger, blond, and rich. Sure, they were both handsome, but Cody had classical features. A broad forehead, deep set brown eyes and a rugged jawline. He looked a bit like the typical rugby player, brawny and wide, but Amelia knew he'd never been much for sports.

Nick was lean and athletic. He had grace and swagger. His near black hair, brows and his occasional afternoon stubble, provided a dark edgy contrast to his light blue eyes. Having come from a poverty-stricken background, Nick never flaunted his triumphant career success. He was always neat and well put together. He had what he needed and that was it. His old junker was proof of that.

Cody sported a salon styled haircut struck through with highlights and jelled to perfection. Wincing, Amelia wondered how much it had cost him. Personally, she preferred Nick's finger combed, slightly tussled hair.

Thinking to treat Nick like a dog who'd pissed on the carpet and had his nose rubbed in it, she'd scoped out clubs frequented by those with elegance and influence. Using her own parent's wealth to gain access, she had gotten exactly what she'd been looking for. Someone she could rub Nick's nose in. It had all backfired.

She'd wanted Nick to feel guilty about what he'd done to her. But now, staring at her ex, it was she who felt ashamed.

Cody's texts and phone messages were all a desperate ploy to get back together. Panicked, Amelia watched him get closer. He hadn't seen her yet. She needed to get rid of him before he ended up crossing paths with Nick.

Pausing here and there, Cody glanced out over the crowd, trying to spot her. A few times his progress was impeded when he stopped to check out a woman's ass or another woman's rack. And here he thought they were getting back together. What a dumbass.

Nudging Amy, Amelia pointed across the party when Cody's back was turned. She didn't need to explain, Amy jumped right on it. "What's he doing here?"

"I told him not to come."

"I got this." Dancing her way across the circle, Amy collided with first Geneva and then Lynn, no doubt telling them to run interference. Watchful, Brent and Kenny both seemed to sense that something was up. They searched the crowd for the girls' sudden unease. Amelia was glad they were here, but unfortunately they couldn't make her invisible. When Cody saw her, everything inside her tensed. The pulsations in her body took a backseat to the loathing and unease she suddenly felt as he made his way toward her.

"Amelia!" Cody threw his arms around her and pulled her close, laying a soft kiss on her cheek.

She pulled back. "What are you doing here, Cody? I told you not to come. What part of *no* don't you get?"

Clasping her hand, he whispered, "Can we talk privately?"

Amelia tried to pull away. "I don't think that's a good idea."

With a sigh, Cody pulled at his ear. He looked at her with big puppy dog eyes from beneath his manicured eyebrows. "You won't return my calls or texts. I haven't had a chance to explain myself. Please just let me say what I came to say."

Behind Cody, Amelia could see Amy shaking her head no, but having never been good with conflict, Amelia relented. "Fine, but just for a minute."

"That's all I ask." Cody grabbed her wrist and tugged her along. She motioned back at Amy who nodded. If she wasn't back soon, her friends would know to come get her.

They found a less crowded area and Cody wasted no time diving in. "Listen, I'm really sorry about how things went down between us. I want to give us another try."

She had to get him out of here before Nick saw. She cut him off. "We want different things."

"I've thought about it more. I think we should give it a try. I was too quick to say no. Let me give it a shot."

Amelia shook her head. "I'm not interested in you anymore."

"Come on, that can't be true. It's only been a few months, you can't be over us already. I miss you, Amelia. Please." His big stupid eyes pleaded.

"Cody, I told you we're done. There's nothing more to say."

A warm arm wrapped around her waist from behind,

startling her so badly she jumped. "Amelia, darling, who's your friend?" When Nick's lips brushed against the shell of her ear, she had to fight not to lean into him. This was the last thing she needed.

Chapter Nine

Nick had been standing with his friends from high school when he first caught sight of the blond-haired man. There were a lot of people at the Fuller's party that Nick didn't know, but something about this dodgy fellow prickled Nick's senses. It was the way he hunted through the crowd. He didn't address anyone and moved through the people like a whisper. Talking to no one, he kept searching out his prey.

The man approached Amelia and she fell into an obligatory hug. Shock was clearly imprinted on her face. So she knew the man, but wasn't necessarily happy to see him here.

"Hey—" his stare never wavering Nick, nudged Gabe—"who's that?"

After a quick glance across the room, Gabe dropped his head back against the wall. "Shit."

"What?" Keeping an indifferent attitude was becoming increasingly difficult with each moment as the blond man grabbed Amelia by the wrist and tugged her away from her friends.

"I think... I think that's her ex," Gabe said, struggling to identify the man from across the room. "Yeah, I'm sure that's Cody."

"I thought you said you never met him."

"I didn't. But I've seen pictures. I mean, come on. She dated the guy for like three years."

Nick mulled that over, wondering if Cody knew about Amelia's sexual preferences. He must. They'd been together for such a long time. It upset Nick to think about any other man with Amelia, but worse still was wondering what Amelia had let Cody do to her. Had he tied her down? Struck her?

Growing angrier by the second, Nick fought to control the sudden impulse to flatten the man. "What's he doing here?"

Kevin and Ed looked over to where Amelia was in a deep discussion with the man.

"I don't know," Gabe replied, "she didn't think he'd actually show up."

"She thought he might?" That was the first he'd heard of it.

Crossing his arms over his chest, Gabe watched his sister. "Yeah, well, he's been texting her for weeks now. Wants to get back together, but she's not interested. He said he was coming tonight, but she didn't think he'd show."

"How did he get into the party?"

"Mom sent out the invitations back when they were still together. Amelia didn't dump him until afterward."

Too many questions flocked Nick's brain.

"Maybe you should see if she's alright," Kevin interjected. They all noticed the way her brows pulled tight over her eyes and how vehemently she was shaking her head at whatever Cody had said to her.

Gabe took a step forward. "Yeah maybe I should."

Nick stopped him with a gentle touch to his arm. With much more restraint than he felt, he pasted a playful smile on his face. "Let me."

Gabe shrugged and gestured for Nick to go first.

Sauntering through the crowd, Nick kept watch on Amelia and her ex, only looking away to use his phone to turn the app off. He wanted stealth. As he approached, he tried to make out pieces of their conversation, but the sound of countless other exchanges drowned them out, until he was almost upon them.

"Cody, I told you. We're done. There is nothing more to say," Amelia was explaining as Nick slid up behind her.

Cody's attention shifted from her as Nick possessively laid his hand on her hip. His soft touch startled her and enraged Cody. "Amelia, darling, who's your friend?" Nick purred into her ear.

Cody stewed as Amelia did the introductions. "This is my ex, Cody, and, Cody, this is," she paused, casting a brief glance up at him, "Nick."

It startled Nick when Cody let out a relieved laugh. "Nick?" he asked triumphantly, his laughter growing, "Your brother's best friend? That Nick?"

Amelia's shoulders slumped, but Nick didn't understand what was so damn funny. Obviously, Amelia had spoken of him to her ex, but why the man would act relieved upon hearing his name was beyond Nick. It was important Cody understood that Amelia belonged to *him.* He'd intended to chase the guy off with a demonstration of possessiveness, but whatever knowledge Cody had about their past relationship shot that plan all to hell.

Amelia patted his hand where it rested on her sequin dress. "Well now that everyone knows everyone I should really get back to my friends. Cody, why don't you check out the buffet, you've come a long way and I'm sure you'll like the cream cheese appetizers. And, Nick, you can go let Gabe know that I'm having a very *pleasurable* evening." Even though her words dripped with hidden meaning, Nick couldn't get over her sudden snub as she deserted them and returned to the dance floor.

One of her friends broke away from the group, probably to fetch a refill. Cody disappeared in the same direction, no doubt hoping to make an ally of her. Jaw clenched, Nick brooded over Amelia's sudden departure.

Whatever she had told Cody about him had her agitated.

She didn't want them near each other, and it was all too clear that she didn't want Cody here at all, which suited him just fine. Half tempted to follow the guy and tell him to hit the road, Nick rocked on his heels, wondering if he should go after Amelia, or her ex.

He needed to get rid of Cody. Amelia was his and he wouldn't have anyone ruin what they'd started.

As he started after her, Amelia seemed determined to ignore him, turning her back to him on the dance floor. Digging into his pocket, Nick reactivated the app, he found and held one of the higher functions on the toy. Punishment for her behaviour. He watched as she dragged her hands through her hair, trying to get a grip on her body. She chanced a glance back to the spot where she had left him. He gave her a smug smile, reminding her anew just who she belonged to tonight.

* * * *

Gabe whistled for a third time and finally succeeded in gaining Nick's attention. He, Kevin, and Ed were all beckoning him back. Nick gave them a quick defeated shake of his head before he made his way toward them.

"What happened?" Kevin asked a bit too eagerly. Gabe knew Kevin had always had a thing for Amelia. Back in eleventh grade, he'd shoved his friend into a locker and threatened him to keep his distance. Now with Amelia fully grown it seemed silly to think of threatening men away from her. She was capable of taking care of herself. Besides he knew she'd chew Kevin up and spit him out if he ever tried approaching her with his juvenile mannerisms.

A chorus of *oohs* and *aahs* had gone up from Kevin and Ed when Nick had put his hands on Amelia, warning Cody off. If it had been any other man touching Amelia, Gabe would have been positively pissed, but he knew he could trust Nick. Of course, Nick had broken Amelia's heart three years ago, but she had been a lovesick pup in need of a good shake back to her senses. After that, Gabe had all the more faith in Nick, knowing full well that he had no interest in Amelia.

"So?" Gabe prodded.

Nick glanced back to where they could occasionally spot Amelia through the swaying ripples of the crowd. "I think I embarrassed her."

The guys laughed.

A moment later, they sobered as they saw Cody striding back toward the dance floor following Geneva. "What about him?"

Nick shrugged. "Couldn't tell. She told him she was done with him."

"Did you believe her?"

"She's given me no reason to think otherwise."

He knew he was being over protective, but he couldn't seem to stop. "Well, we'll just have to keep an eye out."

A passing waiter offered them spring rolls from the tray he carried. They jumped back into their conversation about cars. Occasionally Gabe and Nick would cast an eye toward the dance floor where Cody was trying unsuccessfully to woo Amelia back, but his attempts kept ending with Geneva grabbing up his attention.

Later, while waiting in line at the bar, two ladies in their mid-forties excitedly approached Nick. The first lady had shoulder length brown hair, struck threw with blonde highlights. She had fair eyebrows and sultry dark eyes. The second sported a much shorter cut, the dark hair dye doing little to hide her age as the laugh lines around her eyes and mouth stretched with her eagerness to speak with the twenty-seven-year-old.

"This is the guy I was telling you about," the blonde

started. "Nick, this is my friend Robin."

Nick flashed the women his warm, cunning smile, while Gabe rolled his eyes. Everywhere they went women fell at Nick's feet. It didn't matter their age, race or preference, there was no discriminating when it came to women's mad reactions to him. The rest of their gang teased him about it, but often times Nick slyly deflected the attention as best he could.

"Robin." Nick nodded to the woman before turning to her friend. "How are you, Carol? Keeping up with those exercises I trust?"

Carol must have been a client from the gym. Gabe turned to place their drink orders.

Carol tossed her head of hair and beamed. "Of course. I always do what you tell me to. I was hoping you could help Robin."

"In the spring my husband and I are going to Jamaica and I want to be ready for bikini season," the dark-haired one confessed.

Nick made a leisurely show of casting an examining eye over her, before flashing his wide, white-toothed smile once more. "Well you hardly need my help getting ready to slink into a bikini." The two women giggled like they were in high school. "But if you come by the gym after the holidays I'll see what I can do to help you meet your fitness goals for the New Year. Take Carol's word for it, a resolution with me will be seen through. I don't accept quitters."

Gabe thrust a newly filled glass into Nick's hand and their growing group proceeded away from the busy bar. The two ladies stuck around for a bit longer, before Robin was called away by her husband, and Carol reluctantly went with her. Soon Paige snuck by for a quick kiss before trotting off again with a group of her friends.

A little drunk, Kevin clapped Nick on the back, nearly

spilling his drink. "God, Nick, I don't know how you do it. Do you have any idea what you could have got those two to do?"

Nick frowned. Slightly embarrassed by Kevin, he looked away. Ed reached into his pocket and pulled out a packet of smokes. "Kevin?"

The two headed for the patio.

Meanwhile Nick nodded toward the dance floor. "I don't see them."

Sure enough, Amy, Geneva and Lynn along with a few men, presumably their boyfriends, were still bobbing along to the music. Amelia and Cody were nowhere to be seen.

"I don't like that one bit," Nick continued. Gabe missed his friend's look of outrage. He was already striding into the crowd, searching out his sister.

They found them in the study, which had been converted into a sitting room for tired persons to find a few moments of solace. A few people were scattered through the room. It was mostly filled with the elderly guests that hadn't yet left, and a small number of couples sneaking a quieter moment. Amelia perched on a sofa, while Cody sat in a nearby armchair.

As they approached, he listened in.

"Please, Amelia, I'm begging you to give me another chance. I've given it some thought and I'd like to try it. I'm ready now."

"Look, Cody, I've already told you," Amelia stressed her words, "it's done. No more. Go home. There is nothing more for you here. *Fuuuuuck.*" The word slowly drew from her lips as her body suddenly tensed. She gripped the cushion she was sitting on, her eyes closed, her brows pulled tight as she bit her lower lip. Appalled, Gabe could have sworn it was rapture that crossed her face, he'd seen women fight to prolong that look of ecstasy many times.

A second later it passed. Gabe shook himself, trying to trick his brain into finding some other excuse for that odd behaviour. He dropped down on the couch next to her and draped his arm around her shoulders. "Hey, sis. How's it going?"

She glanced at him, then up at Nick before relaxing into the couch. "It's fine."

"Good, glad to hear it." Ignoring Amelia's death glare, he leaned forward and offered his hand to Cody. "I'm Gabe, Amelia's brother."

Grudgingly, Cody took his offered hand. "I figured as much. I'm Cody. Amelia's boyfriend from school."

Amelia scowled at Cody. "Ex-boyfriend."

"For now." The smile Cody directed at Amelia turned Gabe's stomach.

"Yeah, she's told me all about you." Which was a lie, but if Cody planned to come to their party only to belittle and bully Amelia then Gabe wanted some kind of leverage over the guy. He leaned back into the couch, pretending to be at ease with the situation. "Amelia, why don't you go back and dance with your friends. I'd really like to get to know Cody better."

Amelia looked between the three men. Apparently, she had no intention of leaving her ex with such shitty odds. With his track record for beating on her crushes, ex-boyfriends and basically anyone who looked at her wrong, he didn't blame her.

"You just said you know all about him."

Cody took Amelia's hand. "She's all danced out for the moment."

Gabe reigned in his temper. He didn't like this asshole. "Nick, why don't you take Amelia to get a drink?"

* * * *

Setting his drink down on the little side table, Nick rested his hand on the back of the couch, and played with a strand of her hair. At his naughty tugging, she looked up at him.

"Amelia, come dance with me."

It wasn't a question. It was a command.

Torn, she looked again at Cody, then at Gabe who nodded at her. She knew that if she left Gabe alone with Cody he'd scare him away like he'd done to every interested boy since junior high. She wanted to get rid of Cody, but she could damn well do it herself. She didn't need Gabe fighting her battles for her.

But Nick was another matter entirely. The dark intensity in his eyes spoke heavily, a mixture of possession and violence. No doubt he, too, wanted to pummel Cody, but if he dared to act so brutally, so brashly, everyone would realize their relationship had crossed the border.

"Amelia," he warned again. When she didn't respond, he leaned down to whisper in her ear. "Why are you letting him touch you?"

She was breaking one of their rules. Gulping, she tore her hand out of Cody's grasp. Truthfully, she hadn't even realized Cody was holding her hand. The second Nick had touched the back of her head, all her awareness had been focused on him.

"Good. Now, come and dance with me."

She knew she shouldn't rebuke him, but dancing with him could lead to people talking about them. What if someone figured it out? Knowing the risk of refusing him, she replied, "But..."

Her panties jolted against her. With her brother so close, she fought to keep her face passive, but Gabe still looked concerned.

Nick tugged at her hair again, forcing her to meet his gaze. He gave her one of his wide, warm smiles, meant to reassure. She was pretty sure it was a show for her brother.

Again, his hot breath whispered at her ear, "If we're dancing, I'll give you a break from the toy."

Amelia rocketed up from the couch. "Let's go."

Her quick about-face shocked her brother and left Cody stammering. Nick simply picked up his drink, took her hand and led her away from the sitting area.

Heat from his hand radiated through her fingers. The splendid sensations made her skin tingle and spiked her pulse. Seemingly on a mission, he led her through the crowd, winding their way toward the dance floor. He was so bent on their destination that it looked like one friend leading another, but as his thumb flicked over her knuckles, she couldn't stop the catch in her breath.

Moments before they reached the dance floor, Nick dropped her hand and turned on her. No longer in her brother's company, and not yet in sight of her friends, it seemed he thought now would be the best time for a chat.

"Why didn't you tell me that he might show up here?" he demanded. She opened her mouth to answer, but he cut her off. "And don't you even think about lying to me. Gabe told me you've been texting him. He said you knew he was coming here tonight."

Amelia couldn't help but take a step back as he loomed over her. He was fuming, and frankly, his response shocked her. She'd never expected him to react in such a jealous manner. He propped his fists on his hips, waiting for her to explain Cody's presence while she was still trying to piece it together herself.

A few weeks prior to their break up, she had suggested they introduce some BDSM into their sex life. Cody had been disgusted, and she'd been hurt. She'd put herself out there, and he'd shredded any hope that her fantasy might come true. If Nick hadn't caught her in the act, she certainly wouldn't have been brave enough to venture there again.

But under no circumstance would she consider getting back together with Cody. Nick, or no Nick, Cody had shot himself in the foot as far as she was concerned.

Ah, but Nick was here, and as he stood glaring down at her, she found herself at a loss for an answer. Finally, she managed to stammer, "I really didn't think he'd come. I have no interest in him. I don't give a shit whether he's here or not."

Nick snorted. "Well I do. He looks at you like a piece of meat."

"He can look all he likes. It doesn't change how I feel about him. He won't touch me again." She was convinced of that, but apparently her words didn't soothe Nick.

Just past him, Amelia could see her friends through the swaying people. Frowning with concern, Amy waved her over.

Amelia motioned toward her. "We should keep going."

Nick glanced over, mumbled something and took a step toward her friends. Amelia moved after him and nearly bumped into his back when he abruptly stopped. Twisting to look at her, he pressed two fingers to her chin, briefly lifting her face to meet his whispered words. "You've broken too many rules. I haven't decided what it will be, but there will be a punishment for what's transpired tonight."

There was no point in arguing. With her pulse racing, the word yes slipped from her lips.

"And you will stay away from him. Understood?"

It was on the tip of her tongue to point out that between him and Gabe, Cody wouldn't get near her again, but somehow she knew that wouldn't go over well. She merely submitted. "Of course."

Content, Nick swivelled back toward the dance floor. Exuding confidence, he strutted into her circle of friends. Amelia exchanged a few awkward glances with Amy and Lynn. She tried desperately to hide her ridiculous response to

Nick.

Over the next few songs, the circle expanded. Occasionally someone would leave to get a drink, or a few girls would step away to find the bathroom, but mostly the group grew. A few of Nick's high school friends and a few of his co-workers joined them, Kevin used it as a chance to grind up on Geneva. Sometimes one of Amelia's past co-workers would join the group. At one point Aunt Evelyn glided into their midst to dance a bit with Amelia and her girlfriends before flittering off again.

Nick mostly stuck to the outskirts of the circle, he wasn't a slouch on the dancefloor, but he didn't flaunt his dancing skills. His body moved languidly and Amelia couldn't help but think about how he felt when they were moving rhythmically together. Sparks of jealousy jabbed at her each time a woman approached Nick, gyrating in front of him or against him, but each time Nick managed to foist them off onto one of his mates, who was more than willing to accept Nick's offer.

When the DJ played a slow song, everyone who didn't immediately pair up began to clear off the dance floor. Geneva started to make a b-line for Nick the second the first notes hit the air, but Nick smoothly clasped Amelia's hand and drew her into his arms. Slipping her arms around his neck, she tried to ignore Geneva's pissed off glare.

"We shouldn't be doing this," she complained as his fingers linked behind her waist.

"Whatever. I don't care what everyone else thinks."

You're not the one they're judging, she thought, wincing at the old ache from painful memories in this very venue.

Careful not to bump into other dancers, they began making circles on the floor. The enticing smell of his cologne filled her senses. She had to fight not to lean toward him.

The dampness between her thighs didn't help matters. She

wanted desperately to put some part of him there, his fingers, his tongue, his dick, she didn't care which, but the urge to press against him, to mate with his body consumed her. The sensations he'd sent pulsing through her flesh felt embarrassingly wonderful, but her inner muscles clamped and constricted, demanding that he fill them. *Soon.*

"We said we were going to keep it secret," she insisted. Leaning away from him, she put as much space between their bodies as he would allow. She didn't want people to know that she'd foolishly fallen for him all over again. She knew she was headed down the path of complete and utter heartbreak once more, but there was no need to make it public knowledge.

"Your dad already knows."

"What?" she gasped. "How?"

Nick shrugged and turned with her. "He caught us kissing in the car the other night. And then he and I had a nice little chat."

Amelia groaned. "How did he take it?"

"Much better than I thought he would. I'm not looking forward to when Gabe finds out."

"He's not going to find out."

It seemed as though he was going to dispute the issue, but he remained silent. They rocked to the music, just holding each other. To onlookers they must have appeared like any pair wrapped up in the music, in the holiday magic. Yet sexual tension hummed in her veins.

"Hey, that gift under the tree, I'm not sure you should open it when everyone's around."

Amelia crinkled her brow. "Why not?"

"It's a little revealing."

Amelia thought back to the little box under the tree. It was too small to house lingerie. "What the hell's in it?"

Nick snickered. "Nothing bad."

Silence fell over them as she tried to determine what was in the box.

"It's engraved. You just shouldn't let anyone see what it says. If you don't want people to know about us."

"You're a tease."

He snorted. "Am not."

As the final verse of the song began, Nick pulled her closer, his lips brushing the curve of her ear. "How many times have you come tonight?"

He might as well have turned the toy back on, for his words had the same effect on her body. Another wave of dampness soaked into her panties.

She shuddered.

"How many, Amelia?"

She had to think back. "Five, six I think."

"Mmm," he purred against her hair.

"You haven't been very nice about it." She pouted.

Nick laughed. "I thought I'd been very nice, very considerate. Not to worry, just another half a dozen times should be good."

Amelia's eyes shot wide open. She didn't know how much more she could take before her body melted into a puddle on the floor.

With his lips nearly brushing her neck, he sent shivers tingling across her skin as he whispered, "I've got to be sure you're nice and wet when I enter you tonight."

Her thighs flexed and her fingers knotted in his shirt.

"Careful now." He reached up and unfurled her hand from his shoulder. She followed his gaze to where Gabe was dancing with Paige a few feet away.

A blush crept up to her cheeks. She wanted desperately to tuck her face against Nick's chest to hide her shame. Then she realized if Gabe was here, he'd finished with Cody. The idea that Cody was still in the crowd startled her, and instinctively her gaze began to search for him.

The sensual tone was gone from Nick's voice when he said, "He's over there with Geneva."

Amelia glanced to where Nick indicated and sure enough, there was Cody and Geneva grinding against each other in a slow dance. Amelia chuckled.

Still irritated, Nick asked, "What?"

Amelia shrugged. "It's just fitting."

The song ended and the crowd began bopping along to the next fast-paced tune. Gabe tapped Nick on the shoulder. "Let's go grab a drink?"

No doubt thinking that Nick had done his duty in distracting her while Gabe warned off Cody, Gabe expected them to continue mingling through the party.

Reluctantly Amelia drew herself away from Nick's warmth.

"Thanks for the dance." Nick inclined his head before darting off with her brother. They left her behind like so many times in her childhood, but this time as they walked away, Nick's hand slipped into his pocket. The pulse of the vibrator reminded her that in fact she hadn't been forgotten.

She slipped away with Lynn to grab something to eat and spent the next hour or so dodging Cody. Although she wanted to know what had transpired between Gabe and Cody, she didn't dare risk Nick's wrath. There was no doubt in her mind that Nick noticed if she even glanced in Cody's direction for her pussy got a jolt anytime Cody breached her perimeter. It began to feel a bit like a game to taunt her Dom. Occasionally she'd send him a wicked little smile, growing bolder as the night continued.

She had a bit of a buzz going when the idea struck her. Why did she have to wait until they got home? What was stopping them from fucking right here at the party? She could chase away the memories of her mistletoe disaster and replace them with new memories.

The more the thought tumbled through her mind, the less she questioned it. There were public restrooms on the first and second floor, but on the third floor were the private restrooms, reserved for members and employees of the manor. Her mother brought in almost an entirely different staff. The upper floor would be empty.

As it neared half past twelve, Amy and Brent said their goodbyes to the group. Ditching her clutch and drink with Lynn, Amelia seized her chance to sneak away from the party for a few private minutes. If Nick was really watching her as closely she thought he was, hopefully he'd follow her lead.

Her body had been on edge all night, and she'd ridden the highs and lows that Nick had cast her way. Taking the stairs as quickly as possible in her heels, Amelia hoped to get away before anyone noticed. She avoided the public restrooms on the second floor of the building. She'd frequented them few times over the course of the night with various members of her entourage. It was a brightly painted room with multiple stalls, equipped with fresh crisp towels and various moisturizers, but Amelia craved a moment of solitude. Of privacy.

Amelia came to the top of the second floor and followed the rail around to the third floor staircase. Ignoring the sign that read *employees only,* she continued upward.

The third floor housed the business offices, along with the private bathrooms. She headed down the corridor and turned the corner. Reaching her destination she was about to turn the knob for the restroom when she was stopped by a familiar voice. Just not the one she wanted to hear.

"Going somewhere?"

Chapter Ten

Her heart hammered in her chest as she turned to meet Cody. He leaned in the hallway as his gaze roamed her body. She'd dated him for years, been in love with him, been naked with him, but as his eyes claimed every inch of her figure, she somehow felt violated.

He had been surprisingly persistent. She'd told him no. Gabe had told him no. But still he stood before her.

"Why are you still here?"

"I need to talk to you without anyone listening in. Without your brother and his shadow." He paused as though waiting for permission to speak, but when she didn't respond, he continued. "I was a jerk when you told me what you wanted."

"You pretty much laughed in my face."

He didn't even look ashamed. "I've given it some thought, and I'd like to try it."

Her breath caught. She took a step back as he advanced. "No."

Cody scoffed. "I see what you're doing, you know."

Confused, Amelia shook her head. "What do you mean?"

"With Nick."

How did he know? He'd laughed at her earlier when Nick had shown up, so what had happened? How did he know? And if he knew, did Gabe? Amelia swallowed the lump of fear in her throat.

"He's the reason why you keep saying no." Darkness crept into Cody's blue eyes, turning them cold and chilling. "You're here pining away after him, chasing him around, hoping like hell that your childhood dreams will come true. It's not going to work though. He's plainly not interested in you."

Amelia raised her hand to her lips to stifle her laugh. It came out a cough instead.

"Get some sense. You belong with me, not chasing some guy that's never going to want you. Give it up, let's get back together. I'm agreeing to what you wanted in the first place, all that Dom and sub stuff. All that role playing shit."

Amelia ignored the warning in her head. For years, she'd told herself she wasn't good enough, that Nick never want her. It wasn't true, he did. Maybe not forever, but at least she had right now, and she wasn't about to let Cody ruin it. She squared her shoulders. "I told you no."

He invaded her space. "I'm ready now."

"No," she said again, holding her hand up to warn him back.

He kept coming. "Don't say no to me. I'll show you how good I can be at this."

She jerked backward when he grabbed her wrists. Suddenly realizing what he was really about, why he'd followed her to the secluded space, fear gripped her. She put up as best a fight as she could, but he was so much bigger than she was.

Her back slammed against the wall, almost knocking the breath from her. He manacled her wrists with his hands. Then his lips came crashing down onto hers. Amelia whipped her head to the side, avoiding his wet kiss as best as she could. She squeezed her eyes shut and prayed he'd stop.

In the next moment, she was saved. Nick grabbed Cody from behind and hauled him off of her. With his collar caught in Nick's grip, he was helpless as Nick punched him hard across the face. Cody stumbled backward, wiping the blood from his nose.

"You were warned!" Nick hollered. "Stay away from her."

Nick cast a glance toward her. Drawing in a shaky breath, she forced herself to stand at her full height, determined to prove to Nick she was alright.

Seemingly satisfied, Nick turned his attention back to Cody. "What the hell do you think you're doing?"

"You don't understand." Cody braced himself for another possible attack. "She wants it!"

From behind him, Amelia saw Nick's shoulders bunch, his hands clenched by his sides. Through gritted teeth he muttered, "Rape in the hallway at her parent's party?"

"It's not what it looks like!" Cody insisted.

Hoping to cool their tempers before one of them did something rash, Amelia sidled up to Nick and lightly grasped his hand. "I'm okay, now."

"See!" Cody interpreted her incorrectly. "She's fine. She wanted it."

Amelia felt her own frustration rising as Cody's dense brain didn't comprehend. "I said I'm okay, *now*."

Reaching out, Nick tipped her face up and settled his forehead against hers. "You're sure?"

She nodded.

"Good." Suddenly Nick looped his arm around her waist and dragged her against his body, his right leg nudging her thighs apart to nestle between them. Without a sound, she fell naturally alongside him, her body finding some relief in his nearness. She couldn't control the smile that tugged at her lips.

"Oh my god," Cody breathed, "you're fucking him."

A telltale blush rose up in her cheeks. He'd finally figured it out. She only prayed he didn't blab it all over the party.

"It's not going to work, Amelia. You're just going to have the same problem. When he finds out what you told me he'll bolt for the door, too." Amelia was about to point out that she was the one that had done the dumping, but Cody rambled on. "As soon as he knows your dirty little secret, he'll be disgusted, just like I was."

Amelia's shoulders straightened. He couldn't really be planning to blurt out her private business to the whole world? Not that it was anything new to Nick, but Cody didn't know that. It seemed as though he had no problem telling her secrets. How could she have ever trusted him?

About to give him a tongue-lashing, she was stopped short when Nick pulled his phone from his pocket. For a moment she panicked, worried he'd call Gabe. But when he didn't pull up his contacts, a different fear took over. A fear mixed with anticipation had her begging, "Nick, please not now."

Her eyes were wide as saucers as she watched him flick through the app searching for something specific. She barely caught a glimpse of the word *ecstasy* before he found whatever he was looking for and selected it.

The sensations started all over again and she lurched against him. Her damp panties had already been clinging to her pussy lips, but now as the vibrations started, she couldn't help but rub against Nick's conveniently placed leg. Finally, he was just where she needed him. Unable and unwilling to try to control her body any longer, she grinded her clit against him. Tucking her head into Nick's side, she breathed in his scent as her fingers knotted in the front of his shirt.

For the first time tonight, she didn't have to hide it. She gave herself permission to enjoy what was happening to her body. Moaning, she clung to him, uncaring that her ex watched as she dry humped Nick's person.

"You were saying?" Nick baited Cody.

"What the hell have you done to her? What are you doing?" Cody nearly screamed the words. Amelia could feel his angry stare all over her heated body. She'd never acted this passionately with him. He'd never excited her to this demanding, insistent place, where impulse took over her mind.

"Nick," Amelia moaned his name, unable to contain the plea. Fog wished around her thoughts until all she knew was the burning need to have his body. He was her own special brand of crack, and she was in desperate need of a hit.

"Soon," came his calm reply.

She was partly wild in that moment, losing herself in the knowledge that she was with her Dom. He would protect her, cherish her, and bring her pleasure. All she needed to do was submit.

"Amelia belongs to me now," Nick explained, "and I don't share."

While Cody stood gaping like a fish, Nick moved his hand down over her body until it settled firmly on her ass, pulling her more closely to him, claiming her once more. "Amelia?"

She whimpered.

"Amelia, Cody's leaving now. Is there anything more you'd like to say to him?"

He sounded so haughty, yet when she looked at him, he wasn't smiling. Amelia instinctively knew what Nick wanted in that moment. He wanted to make Cody understand it wasn't just fucking. Nick had fulfilled the role that Cody himself had declined. No threat Cody could make would frighten Nick away. Without so much as a farewell glance toward her ex, she replied loudly, "No, Sir."

"There you have it. Now get lost." The warning tone in Nick's voice was back, the same dark tone he took with her when she misbehaved. She smiled weakly and pressed a little kiss to his rib cage.

"Fuck you," was Cody's final rebellious stand before pivoting and marching back down the hall.

Before Cody turned at the elbow of the upper floor, Nick threw out the last word. "Nah, I'm going to fuck Amelia."

Grateful, she looked up at him again. "Yes, please."

* * * *

Nick fumed.

The impulse to stomp after Cody and put him through the nearest wall was only slightly over ridden by the urge to dominate Amelia. Glancing down at her, he worked his jaw back and forth, attempting to calm his anger.

"What the hell were you doing alone with him?"

Amelia didn't answer. Using all his self-restraint, Nick peeled her body from him and set her aside. "I asked you a question."

A beautiful flush filled Amelia's skin. She was in bad need of sexual relief. He'd pushed her hard tonight, making demands of her that primed her precious, fertile young body.

She lowered her lashes. "He followed me."

"Look at me. What were you doing up here?"

Raising her chin, she avoided his gaze for a moment, before finally finding the bravado to meet his eye. She knew he was angry and her own temper sparked. From across the wide hallway, he could still sense when her body tensed.

"I was looking for the loo." Her eyebrow rose, challenging him to question her.

"Why not use the public one like everyone else? Coming up here left you vulnerable to him."

She crossed her arms under her chest, unconsciously giving her breasts extra oomph they didn't need. Mad as he was he still couldn't stop himself from looking.

"I wasn't thinking about him. I wanted some privacy. I was..." She dropped her gaze again. "I was hoping you'd follow me."

Nick's pulse quickened. He struggled to keep control. "Look at me."

Again she hesitated.

"You've broken so many rules tonight what's one more, right?" His voice was stern, but inwardly it excited him to think of doling out punishment to Amelia. The more she ran, the more he wanted to chase her. The more she fought him the more aroused he became.

Amelia peered up at him from beneath her lashes, but her head remained tucked.

"Where's this washroom?"

Her head whipped up so fast, a smile spread wide over her features. She took his hand and led him down the hall to the second last door.

The room he followed her into was extravagant. White tile floors gave way to systematically placed pillars, which held up a salt and pepper marble counter top that stretched across the width of the entire room. Above it a mirror loomed from the counter to the ceiling, reflected within it were the deep twin sinks. Red automated sensors winked at them from the tall grey soap dispensers and faucets, triggered by the motion sensing lights that had come on. Against the opposing wall, two black stall doors blocked off the toilets. The blinds where pulled shut on the window.

Amelia barely had the door closed when Nick slammed her back against it, diving deep into her mouth. God, he'd wanted to kiss her all night! The secrecy was killing him. He wanted to be able to put his hand on the small of her back, he wanted to kiss her temple when she said something witty, he wanted to feed her morsels off his plate and feel the tip of her tongue grazing his fingers.

Finally, he had her.

His fingers raked her scalp, dragging through her soft hair, as his tongue stroked over hers. He felt as though he were no better than Cody in that moment, mauling her like a bear, but when she moaned her approval and began running her fingers down his chest, he knew she wanted this.

For moments, they stayed like that, kissing against the door. He couldn't seem to drag his mouth away. When common sense finally edged in, he mumbled as he pulled back, "You are so delicious."

Eyes closed, Amelia smiled, her body rolling back to utilize the stability of the door.

He grabbed her chin, almost a little too roughly, but he couldn't seem to help himself. "Darling, what did I say about looking at me?" Her lashes bolted open. "Keep those eyes on me, princess."

"Yes, Sir."

Skimming the palms of his hands down her sides, he let the sequins nip at him. By the time he reached the hem, his flesh tingled. He traced his fingers back and forth beneath the edge of the material, casing the thighs he longed to part.

"Let's see how well this little bullet worked. Spread your legs, just a bit."

She did as he asked, inching her thighs apart.

"Good. Right there." Slowly he drew his fingers up her inner thigh. Her skin was dangerously heated, indicating that the vibrator had done its job. But it wasn't until he neared the apex of her thighs that he discovered just how well it had worked.

Her thighs were wet. Her panties were drenched.

Nick clenched his teeth to hold back the groan that threatened to rip from his throat. He dipped his head near her shoulder and whispered into her ear, "So wet."

"Yes."

"Must have been embarrassing."

"Yes."

"Uncomfortable."

"Yes."

He ran his fingers along the edge of her panties, causing her to flinch. "So, you're a little ready?"

"Yes." This time her answer was little more than a hoarse moan.

"For what?" he asked innocently, placing a kiss to her earlobe.

"Cock."

He nipped her neck. "Whose?"

She squirmed. "Yours."

"You want me to fuck you?"

"Yes," she breathed with an edge of impatience.

He straightened. "Say please."

Her eyes met his. Her tongue darted out to moisten her lips. "Please fuck me."

"Take the panties off and hand them to me."

She bent to remove them. A second later, he held them and laughed. "They're soaked."

He withdrew the vibrator and tossed it into the nearest sink before dropping the panties on the countertop. "Turn around, and place your hands on the door."

When she stood with her back to him, he reached past her to lock the door. Once he'd ensured their privacy, his hand found the hem of her dress. He inched it up over her bare ass and bunched it to keep it hanging on her hips. He skimmed his fingers over the cheeks of her ass. He itched to spank her delicate bottom, but knew for everything she'd put him through tonight her punishment had to be much more severe. He'd have to come up with something, but not tonight.

He traced the crack of her ass, dropping his fingers lower until they found her swollen, soaking pussy lips. He parted her, placing his fingertip at her warm, wet entrance. She bucked backward, trying to impale herself on his fingers. She wanted relief from the sweet torment he'd inflicted on her tonight, but he wouldn't give it to her, not that easily. She bucked and moved with him as he slid his digits against her opening. Watching her struggling with her body's need, he suddenly decided on her punishment. But he would dole it out tomorrow. Right now, he needed to fuck her. Hard and fast, pushing them both to release.

And just that suddenly, he pulled away from her. She cast a glance over her shoulder, determined it seemed to obey his latest command.

"Hop up on the counter." He patted the cold stone surface.

Cheeky as ever, she smirked and quickly complied. As her ass hit the counter, she let out a sharp gasp when the hard marble shocked her warm flesh.

Nick couldn't contain his laughter. He shook his head at her before grasping her knees and dragging her to the edge. Without her panties, and nearly toppling from the counter, she was just where he wanted her. Exposed and ready.

When the night began, he never thought he'd end up screwing in a bathroom, but now, he really didn't think he could wait.

He freed his rigid cock from his dress pants. Taking her hand, he wrapped it around himself, wordlessly asking her to stroke him. "It'll have to be fast."

She nodded. Game as always.

He pushed her hand aside and approached the counter. She wrapped her legs around his waist and arched her back, inviting him into her body. He positioned himself at her entrance and wiggled the head around, coating himself in her juices. Then he slowly pushed the tip, just the tip into her.

She groaned, letting her head lull back.

As much as it pained him, he pulled out and waited for her attention. When he didn't continue their joining, she looked at him. "You keep forgetting the rules, sugar. Eyes on me."

"Right," she muttered before pushing her pussy toward him. She didn't remove her gaze from his.

He knew he shouldn't, but he couldn't avoid teasing her. With a frown, he said, "I'm not sure if you really want this."

Amelia basically growled her frustrations. For a second, her eyes drifted away, but she quickly brought them back, eager to please him. "Yes, I do."

He rubbed himself in her heat and naughtily taunted, "I don't think you do." She moaned again, prompting him to position once more for penetration. He lowered his face inches from hers and whispered, "Prove it. Amelia. Beg me for it."

She winced and tried to impale herself on his dick. He denied her. She could fight him all she wanted but he knew she needed him to take control. He'd withhold even if it killed him. His cock swelled and his balls drew tight. He needed to bury himself deep within her. He'd been aching for her all night, but he'd wait until she gave in.

He arched an eyebrow.

She surrendered. "Please, please fuck me. I'm begging for it. I need you, please, Sir, only you."

He drove in deep. They moaned in unison. She was so wet; her body hugged him into her. Hooking her legs with his elbows, he brought her ass off the counter. Using her hands behind her to brace for his every thrust, Amelia lifted her hips and moved with him.

She tossed her head back. "I can't take it. It's so deep."

"You can and you will," he panted. Her slippery heat enfolded him, squeezing him tight. His body was building toward his climax when he felt his phone vibrate against his thigh, a ring tone played out loudly a millisecond later. It was Gabe's ring tone.

She stopped, breaking their rhythm. "Your phone."

"Ignore it."

He plunged into her, making her forget. His lips came crashing down on hers, invading her mouth as he took her body. The heat was building; he could feel sweat beginning to form at the base of his neck. He pulled back, wanting to see her breasts, but the damn dress was in the way. He had to be content with watching her cleavage bouncing with his every thrust. He went faster.

Her moans began a steep crescendo. She was close. He was desperate to feel those warm inner walls spasm around him.

His phone rang again. Gabe's timing had always sucked. Amelia was about to open her mouth, no doubt to remind him of his phone. He snorted. She snapped her mouth shut. They had to hurry up and get back down stairs, before...

A hasty knock sounded at the door.

"Oh, god," Nick snarled, "What?" He tossed the word at the locked door.

"Nick! It's Gabe. I can't find Amelia." Gabe's panicked voice came barreling through. "You've got to help me find her."

All motion in the bathroom had stopped. Amelia's eyes were wide, but not once did they leave his face.

"I'm busy!" he shouted.

The doorknob jiggled.

Nick's heart pounded in his chest, his breath pulled in harshly against his nostrils. "Don't you dare try to open that fucking door!"

"We've got to find her!" Gabe shot back, but the doorknob stilled.

Nick was thankful that she had left her purse somewhere else. If Gabe had dialled it and heard it ringing from within the bathroom walls, Nick would have been a dead man.

"I'll give you five minutes."

Amelia struggled in his arms, fighting to be put down. "Where do you think you're going?"

Dread was clear on her features as she shushed him and motioned to the door.

"He already knows I'm in here." Nick refused to lower his voice, but when she continued to try to climb off the counter, despite the fact that he was still buried inside her, Nick knew he had to do something. There was no way he was stopping now.

Reaching to the adjoining wall, he turned on the hand dryer, which noisily rumbled to life.

"Oh great, that'll buy us what? Twenty seconds?"

Nick arched a brow. "Not enough time huh?"

She glared.

"I'm not letting you down. We're finishing this." To prove his point, he dropped his fingers to rest on her engorged clitoris. Her body bucked. He rubbed it harder. She had to bite her lip to keep from crying out. Her inner muscles clenched around him.

"I can't be that quiet," she sobbed.

"You're going to be," he commanded.

The hand dryer turned off.

He pulled out and thrust into her again. He'd have to build up their momentum again. It'd be so much harder to get her to let go with her brother standing right outside. He repeated the motion. She bit harder into her lip, her fingernails digging into his forearm.

This wasn't going to work.

Nick undid his tie and slipped it from around his neck. Amelia looked at him in question, but refused to speak, which was fine by him. He leaned forward as though he meant to kiss her. She was ready, eager to receive his kiss. Her lips parted and he shoved the silk material into her mouth.

Shocked, she reared back, but was too late. He'd already wrapped it around her head and secured it in the back. She reached up to untie it.

"Oh no you don't." He grabbed her hands and used one of his to lock her in a firm grip. She fought him. Using their linked hands, he pushed against her back, dragging her across the counter, hauling her body to him after all her failed fighting.

He loomed over her, feeling her nipples pucker against her dress, rubbing at him through their clothing. Gingerly, as though he had all the time in the world, he kissed the curve of her neck. He could feel her hair and traces of his necktie dangling against his cheek.

She panted into the material. She was turned on by the added restraint. Hotly, he spoke into her ear, "That's better. Now, spread your legs, link your ankles behind my back and fuck me like the good little slut you are."

Her pussy gushed. Her body undulated beneath him, thrusting her breasts more fully against him. She did as she was told. Her thighs parted wide before she ran her high heels down his back and linked her ankles as directed.

"Good. Now move."

She did.

Her hips propelled up, and he thrust his thick cock into her, over and over and over, until their rhythm became frenzied. She fell back, her body stretched across the counter as he dominated. Her head sunk against the mirror, banging slightly with each thrust. He held her fast, one hand awkwardly binding her wrists, the other he used to guide her hips to help her keep pace.

He dug his nose into her neck to inhale her intoxicating scent, but all he could smell was the spicy sexual odour that rolled off them in waves. He grunted. Balls tightening, he gave up the fight against his impending release and ordered, "Now, come for me, now."

She did.

Wildly she bucked beneath him, moaning helplessly into the makeshift gag until everything in her went lax. Nick bit into her neck, stifling his noise as he emptied into her. His body shuddered and sagged against her. He inhaled sharply, trying to cool his racing pulse.

When he released her wrists, she sighed and hugged him to her. In the back of his mind it briefly registered he hadn't used a condom. Fuck it. They'd deal with that later.

He untied the gag and withdrew from her body. After he fastened his pants, he went to the sink and turned on the water to cover their voices.

"Stay in here and give me at least ten minutes to get him back downstairs." As he spoke, he rinsed the vibrator, shook it off and slipped it into his pocket. He added his tie to the opposite pocket where he kept his cell phone. It was no doubt blinking at him with two missed calls from Gabe.

"Okay."

"And when I go out there I want you to wait in one of those stalls. I don't want him to see you in the mirror."

"Okay."

About to move away from the tap to allow it a chance to shut off, he was stopped by her gentle touch. "Thank you."

Nick sent her a playful smile. "Anytime."

Her thumb caressed his knuckles. "I mean for stopping him." She glanced away. "I was terrified, and I really don't want to think about what would have happened if you hadn't followed me."

"Hey—" he pressed two fingers beneath her chin and forced her to look at him—"you belong to me now. No one else touches you. Understood?"

She smiled. "Yes, Sir."

Nick let the tap shut off. He didn't want to think about what would have happened either. It was over now, and he was pretty sure Cody would give up the fight. Amelia hopped off the counter and reached for her panties. He snatched them away before she could grab them.

She opened her mouth to protest—but with a smile tugging at his lips, he shushed her. Shoving the wet panties into the pocket containing the vibrator—Nick made for the door. He motioned to the stalls. "Hustle."

She glared at him, but did as she was told.

Mentally preparing himself—Nick took a deep breath before inching the door open. To his surprise, he didn't end up face to face with Gabe.

Leaning a few feet down the hall—Gabe was playing a game on his phone. He glanced up, but didn't bother to straighten as Nick came toward him. "Oh yeah, I can see finding Amelia is really urgent."

They fell into a casual stride as they made their way down the hall and around the corner. "Who were you fucking in there?"

"I wasn't."

"Oh please, I know that look. Your hair is all messed up, you're way too smug," Gabe pointed out when they descended the first set of stairs, "and your tie is missing."

"It's none of your damn business."

"It wasn't Carol, was it?"

"Who the fuck is Carol?"

"The chick from the gym, she was throwing herself at you tonight."

Oh Carol. "Who I fuck and where I fuck is none of your business." *Besides you really don't want to know.*

"Don't have a fit. Come on, let's find my sister."

"Why are you suddenly looking for her?"

"Someone saw Cody leave, and now I can't find Amelia. I hope she didn't go off with him." They came to the first floor and started searching through the remaining people. No wonder Gabe was worried, the crowd had thinned considerably. Finding someone shouldn't be that hard.

"Cody left?"

"Yeah."

"Good." Gabe started to rush off, but Nick grabbed his shoulder. "Where are you going?"

"Maybe we should split up."

That pissed Nick off. "No way! You dragged me down here, away from very pleasurable company. We're not going to split up."

When Amelia came down, Nick wanted to be there to ensure that Gabe didn't put two and two together. If she came down looking all flushed and as thoroughly fucked as she had been, Gabe would know and then Cody wouldn't be the only one who ended up with a bloodied nose. He'd seen Gabe's temper snap when it came to Amelia, and he didn't plan to be on the receiving end of that. Hell, he'd helped Gabe beat the shit out of guys for making a derogatory remark.

You bound, gagged and fucked his sister in a washroom. He's going to kill you.

"Maybe she went out for fresh air," Nick suggested, hoping to get a little himself.

Even though it was doubtful, they checked anyway. When they came back inside, they spotted her. She stood chatting with Lynn and Geneva on the dance floor. Nick sent up a silent thank you prayer. She didn't look as dishevelled as he'd left her. She took her purse and her drink back from Lynn.

Gabe stomped up to her. "Where the hell have you been?"

Imp like, Amelia turned to them with a bright smile as though she was about to purposely divulge their secret.

Fearful, Nick tried to get a read on her mood. Her head swung to one side as she let her gaze wander down his body. Wrapping her tongue around her straw to suck up the booze in the cup had Nick fighting not to get hard all over again. The little brat was teasing him. He tried to silence her with his frown, but in front of Gabe, there was little he could do.

She tilted her head the other way and looked at Gabe. Her smug smile stuck in place.

Deciding to help ward off any thoughts they'd been together, Nick threw out the first accusation. "Are you drunk?"

"No!" she scoffed then swatted at him with her free hand, her drink sloshing in the other. Then she leaned closer, like she was telling them a secret. "Maybe a little."

He knew it was a lie. Amelia was completely sober.

"For shit's sake, Amelia." Gabe grasped her arm. "It's time to get you home before you do something stupid again this year."

Everyone paused. Lynn and her boyfriend stared wide eyed as the scene began to unfold. Regret flashed across Gabe's features, but it was too late.

Amelia ripped out of Gabe's embrace, thrusting her drink at him. "By all means, Gabe, hustle me out of here before I embarrass anyone further."

She had only gone a few feet when Gabe called out to her. "Amelia, wait!"

Eyes shimmering, she turned on him. "No, you wait!" She pointed a finger at his chest, her drunken charade vanished. "You need to let me make my own mistakes. Back off and give me my fucking freedom."

Nick's chest tightened. *Mistake.* She was referring to him.

Surprised at her own outburst, she blinked, the tears spilling over her eyeliner-rimmed lashes. Nick looked at his shoes. He itched with the need to soothe her pain.

"We're not children anymore," she whispered before walking away.

By the time they'd gathered Paige, said goodbye to the Fullers, and retrieved their coats, the cab that had taken Amelia home had already returned. It was nearly two in the morning when Nick and Gabe made it home. The ride had taken nearly twice as long on the way back, the pavement slick with accumulating snow and ice.

There was no hope in repairing what had happened. It would have to wait until morning.

Nick took out his phone and sent her a quick text. He

needed her to know he was still thinking about her. *I'm glad we enjoyed your present tonight. Tomorrow there will be a penalty, though.*

His phone dinged from the shelving around the head of the bed while he stripped out of his formal clothing and hung them up. He donned his pajama bottoms and crawled between the sheets before checking her response.

Looking forward to it!

Chapter Eleven

After switching on the coffee pot, Amelia set a few bowls and spoons on the table. Predicting that her little cousins would be the first up, she put a few sugar-laced cereals on the table and pulled the milk from the fridge.

She filled her own bowl with one of the cereals and topped it off with milk. She'd only had a few spoonfuls before she heard the basement door open, and Nick sauntered down the hall into the kitchen.

"Hey." He nodded to her after a quick glance into the breakfast nook. Mouth full, Amelia saluted him with her spoon. She watched as he gathered a few things from the kitchen. "Coffee?"

"Yes, please."

He pulled down two yellow mugs from the cupboard and filled them each with coffee. Leaning over the counter, he asked, "Creamer?"

Amelia nodded. "And sugar."

Shaking his head, Nick frowned at her. Amelia simply ate her cereal and watched him prepare her coffee. Black and steaming, he set his at the end of the table next to where she was sitting and placed hers in front of her bowl.

Like it was a morning ritual, Nick leaned down and surprised her with a kiss on the mouth, stopping her mid-thank you.

Nick returned to the kitchen to prepare his own breakfast, while Amelia sat, puzzled, staring blankly at the steam rising from his coffee.

Thinking back on last night, she realized how unprepared she'd been going into the evening. Surprises awaited her at every turn, making her question all her decisions. She'd felt empowered by her secret love affair with Nick and it had made her cocky, yet friends and family alike had proved to her they all still felt empathy for her disastrous judgment three years ago.

But Nick had taken care of that. Instead of dwelling on their sympathetic comments and pitied glances, she'd been shuddering with pleasure and attempting to hide it. He'd taken every precaution to help her enjoy her evening. Rather than reciprocate, she had burdened his night. She really should have told Nick that Cody might show up.

She really should have trusted him.

But with their problematic past, how could she?

A few minutes later, Nick joined her at the table, pulling her from her musings. His bowl was filled with a healthy bran cereal covered in freshly sliced bananas.

Chasing the few remaining loops around the perimeter of her cereal bowl, Amelia mumbled, "How can you eat that stuff?"

"Pardon?" Nick asked while pouring milk over his breakfast.

She motioned with her hand. "It's not even food. How can you eat that?"

Nick scoffed. "Talk about not food, yours is artificial flavours and sugar. It's totally processed."

"No, it's not."

After taking a spoonful, Nick reached across the table for the box that contained her chosen cereal. Proving his point, he read off the first few ingredients followed by a list of things he could barely pronounce. "See, not real food."

Unwilling to give up, Amelia persisted. "Yours looks like something a cow would eat."

With a smirk, Nick slowly shook his head, amused by her need to argue the point.

"No one else here is willing to eat it," Amelia insisted while setting aside her spoon and lifting her bowl. "You have to bring your own. You must have horrible taste." Lifting the bowl to her lips, Amelia drank her sugar-laced milk.

Nick's stare darkened as he watched her lick any remnants from her lips. "You're wrong." Leaning back in his chair, he let his lazy stare travel down her body. At length, he replied, "I have excellent taste."

Amelia squirmed under his gaze. The effect it had on her was so potent, he may as well have been stroking her. To distract herself, she took a sip of coffee. Nick's gaze dropped back to his cereal. Her body slumped in relief, but when she released her mug, Nick grabbed and held her hand. He brushed his fingers over her knuckles.

Silently he ate his cereal and bananas, while she sipped her coffee, their hands intertwined on the table.

"What have you got planned today?"

Amelia sighed. "Nothing. It's nice to be on break. Nowhere to go, nothing to do."

Nick flashed a playful grin. "I could help you with that."

She met his gaze and flirted back. "I'm pretty sure you already have been."

When he didn't look away, Amelia felt her face begin to flush. She broke eye contact first. Dropping her gaze, she used her free hand to trace the curve of her mug's handle. "Even though it's a lot of work I'm going to miss school."

"You're almost done though, right? Gabe mentioned you have a job lined up for the summer," Nick said before taking another bite.

Loving the warmth of his hand, Amelia settled into her seat. "Nothing fancy. I'm going to help Mom out with the business for the wedding season. I'm applying to a few qualified interior designers over the summer and hopefully will find someone to work under come the fall."

"Sounds like a solid plan."

Amelia shrugged. "Once I gain some experience, I can work on branching out on my own, starting my own business. That is if I haven't found a company I enjoy working for. Oh, and Dad wants me to decorate the interior of the new floor model."

"That's cool. Gabe is looking for an office space. Once he decides on one to rent, maybe you could help him out, too."

She grinned. "Trust me, I've already got ideas on that one."

Nick laughed. In the distance, they heard the grind of a snowplow. As it moved closer, the noise grew louder. They had a long driveway, but the snowplow was so heavy Amelia knew it would have woken someone else up.

After eating the last bit of his cereal, Nick changed the topic. "So you'll be hanging around the house today? Or do you have plans with the girls? Or with anyone..."

He let that last thought hang there. It was rare to see Nick unsure of himself.

With a smile, she reassured him. "I'm just going to be hanging around."

With his cereal bowl empty, he set aside his spoon and took a drink from his mug. Placing his forearms on the table, he leaned forward. Bluntly he spat out, "I didn't use protection."

She didn't look at him when she replied, "I know."

"You'll let me know?" She wavered, drawing his scrutiny. "Amelia, this is serious. I need to know."

Glancing up, she waved away his concern. "The timing is off. I'm sure it's fine."

"Either way, you'll tell me?"

"Yeah. Of course." She wanted to ask him if she should bother making an appointment with her doctor to get back on the pill. If they'd be together that long. Her school was close enough that she could come back to visit plenty, and he could drive out to see her. But was that the kind of relationship they had?

"About last night..."

Amelia blinked a few times, unsure of what he might say. Was he going to ask about Cody, or would he tell her what her punishment would be? That thought made her quiver. However, it was chased away by memories of the end of the night. Her stomach knotted. Surely he wouldn't bring up her argument with her brother. Or worse, the incident that took place three years ago beneath the mistletoe.

"Look..."

Three noisy voices were followed by rapid footfalls. Amelia yanked her hand from Nick's hold. Getting up, she cleared her dishes, but she could feel Nick tracking her movements even after her cousins came barreling into the room. Lauren, Camille, and Anthony scrambled into various chairs around the table and began pouring their cereal. Amelia was just finished washing her dishes and placing them in the dry tray when Uncle Jacob came around the corner, his wide mouth open with a drowsy yawn.

"Morning, Jake," Nick called from the breakfast nook.

Uncle Jacob nodded at each of them in turn, while scratching at his pajama top. "Morning," he muttered around another yawn before reaching into the cupboard for a coffee mug. After his first sip of coffee, he let out a soul-wrenching groan.

Nick chuckled. "Rough night?"

"I guess so."

Going to the couch, Amelia curled up and turned on the electric fireplace. Still she could sense Nick's gaze as though he wanted to join her cuddled up on the couch. She ignored him to the best of her ability.

Gabe joined them all a few minutes later, mimicking Uncle

Jacob's desperation for caffeine.

Getting up to put his dishes away, Nick nearly had his pants pulled down when Lauren tugged on them. Barely balancing his bowl while yanking his pajamas back into place around his hips, Nick turned his gaze on the little girl. Uncle Jacob and Gabe snickered. Nick tried for patience. "Yes, Lauren?"

Innocent to the fact she'd nearly exposed him, Lauren turned her big baby blues on him. "Will you build a snowman with me and Camille today?"

It was Amelia's turn to snicker. She knew what that meant. Nick would spend the afternoon building a snowman to the contradicting instruction of two eight-year-old girls. Nick looked at the other two men, Amelia assumed it was a ploy for help, but soon learned the truth.

"Of course I will."

The girls squealed their excitement. Gabe and Uncle Jacob flinched. Gabe nearly spilled his coffee. Uncle Jacob instantly scolded. "Girls! Daddy has a headache today. No yelling and definitely no squealing."

"I second that." Gabe hightailed it out of the room, Nick's laughter following him. Bypassing the breakfast area, Gabe took a seat across from Amelia and sipped at his coffee.

Still furious at him for how he'd ended her evening, Amelia glared.

Nick stood nearby, coffee mug in hand, as Gabe sheepishly started his apology. "I'm sorry. I shouldn't have said anything last night. It wasn't my place."

"No, it wasn't," she said curtly.

"I shouldn't have brought it up. What happened that night—"

"Is in the past." Amelia glanced at Nick.

Gabe continued, "Yeah, well I'm still sorry, I—"

Cutting him off again, Amelia shoved up from the couch.

"How about we just leave it at you're sorry, and we won't talk about it again."

Ignoring them all, Amelia left the room. Deciding to hide out in her room for a few hours until her grandparents woke, she hurried to the stairs, but not before hearing Gabe and Nick's muted conversation.

"She's still pissed."

"Do you blame her?"

Gabe growled. "No. I promised myself I wouldn't bring it up, the last thing she needed was a reminder. God, that was stupid. My mom will skin me alive if she doesn't come back from school this year."

Like a promise, Nick said, "That won't happen."

"How can you be so sure?"

Nick paused. Amelia ensured her footfalls were silent as she crept up the stairs. "Last night was just a painful reminder. Amelia's right. If we ignore it, maybe it'll go away, like it never happened."

Gabe's next words cut right through her. "I wish it hadn't happened."

Amelia waited to hear Nick's response, but after a long minute, he asked Gabe about his plans for the day. About half an hour later, she watched from her bedroom window as they threw their gym bags in Gabe's trunk and drove off.

Chapter Twelve

"We should ask for a carrot for its nose!" Lauren huffed as she struggled to push the growing snowball along the ground.

Nick was building the bottom ball for the snowman while Camille kept shouting, "Bigger!"

Camille ran over to help her twin. While the two girls rolled the ball, Nick wondered how they kept roping him into these things. When it came to women and children, he really needed to learn how to flat out say no.

With the girls distracted, he could quit on the idea of *bigger*. He planted the enormous white ball in the middle of the yard and started working on the head. Eventually the girls gave up. Nick hefted their middle ball onto the first one. Lauren took over rolling the head. Camille began working on a snow puppy to keep the snowman company.

Nick smiled to himself as Camille made little woofing noises. She reminded him so much of Amelia, creative and clever. Lauren favoured Gabe's quiet, no nonsense work-till-it's-done attitude.

Lauren left the head near Nick's feet. "I'm going to get a carrot!"

Nick packed snow between the first two balls to keep them anchored together before he mounted the head.

Lauren came trotting back through the snow.

Taking a step back, Nick inspected the snowman. It remained rooted in place. "Where's the carrot?"

"Amelia's bringing it."

A few minutes later, the door opened again. With a carrot in one hand and a toque in the other, she joined them in the yard. "That looks great, guys!" She circled the pile of snow. "I bet Uncle Chris has a scarf, or something we can use to make a scarf, in the garage."

Nick couldn't pull his eyes away from her. The wind tugged at her brown tresses and the cold bit at her cheeks. She looked adorable when her cheeks were red. Thinking of Amelia and red cheeks had Nick thinking about the activities they'd been sharing lately. Adorable wasn't what he thought of when he imagined reddening her other cheeks. Just that quickly he was fighting a boner. "I'll come with you. I'm sure we can find something to use for the eyes."

The girls nodded their agreement, but quickly turned back to the growing kennel their snowman was accumulating.

The garage was silent. It was unusual for Chris to be in the house. He loved tinkering in the garage, but everyone always spent the day after the big Christmas party holed up in the house. It was a recovery day reserved for board games and movies. A low-key afternoon. Today everyone had slept late. Christmas Eve was tomorrow so Evelyn and Sally were double checking all the holiday supplies and buying any last minute gifts. Jacob and Chris were nursing hangovers. Gabe was out with Paige. Anthony was playing video games, while Tammy and George retired for their afternoon nap.

Setting her mittens on the workbench next to the gloves he'd pulled off, Amelia rummaged through the toolbox. "This might work." She held up a couple of washers to examine them in the dim light that spewed through the grungy window.

Brushing his body along the length of her back, Nick used his arms to trap her against the bench. Even through the layers of clothing, he felt her melt. "Yeah, this might just work."

* * * *

"What do you think you're doing?"

With one hand, Nick spun her around. His eyes were dark as he leaned toward her. The garage was cold. His breath misted in the air. "We need to discuss your punishment."

She rubbed the washers together in her palm, giving herself a distraction. Her heart raced as the seconds ticked by. Nick had taken to his role as Dom. Last night had proved that. Making her wear the vibrator had been creative and unexpected. He had been controlling. He had never forced her to do anything, yet he had completely dominated her responses. He'd made her excited, made her wet, made her beg for him. The memory of his tie made her mouth water.

"Look at me."

She glanced up, looking just beyond his shoulder. A part of her resented how easily she succumbed to him. How easy she had always been for him. She told herself that was the reason she fought his authority. Gathering her courage, she swung her gaze to his.

"Do you know what rules you broke?"

"Yes."

"Tell me."

"I didn't dance when you asked me to."

He edged closer. "You weren't asked. You were told."

For a second her line of sight wavered. "Right. I disobeyed."

"When else?"

"In the bathroom. I struggled after we were interrupted."

"And?"

Thinking, Amelia wet her lower lip.

On the bench beside her, Nick's fingers curled and uncurled around the edge of the table. His jaw tensed. "You were kissing Cody."

Her eyes widened. "No. I didn't want that."

"He was holding your hand." Nick's voice was little more than a growl.

Amelia held up her hands. "I was trying to get rid of him. I didn't want him there. I didn't want that. *I don't want him.*"

"You should have let me deal with it the first time instead of brushing me off. What did you—" The question was left hanging between them. He didn't need to ask it. She knew. He wanted to know what she'd told Cody about him. He shook his head. "We agreed to be exclusive. You let another man touch you, intimately. And you disobeyed, multiple times."

Amelia was ready to argue about Cody, but she bit her tongue. This was more than the game. He was upset by what had happened last night. Was their relationship deeper than she'd thought? Nick moved on before she could question it.

"How many times did you come last night?"

"I lost track. A lot." The memory of it still weakened her body.

He traced her lips with his thumb. "I watched you come from across the room. Each time you fought against it, each time you struggled not to show it on your face. The pleasure overwhelmed you. In my head, I could hear you panting. I could smell your release. I felt the pull of your body."

She whimpered.

"Yesterday you came, over and over and over."

Amelia closed her eyes, relishing the feel of his fingertips as they played across her cheekbones, as they dipped down the column of her throat.

"Today you will not come."

Her lashes flicked open.

His crooked smile spanned his face. "You heard me. No matter what I say, no matter what I do to you, you will not come. Your punishment will end at midnight tonight." As he spoke, he slipped the buttons free on her coat. He eased her sweater's zipper down. His breath warmed her lips before his own rubbed against hers. His fingers slithered beneath the hem of her shirt. His touch warmed her belly before gliding under the wire of her bra.

She moaned when he cupped her breast, he took advantage, his tongue sweeping into her mouth. Pushing onto her tiptoes, she eagerly participated, her fingers running through his hair, pulling him closer to her.

His free hand found the hem of her yoga pants and dipped beneath it. He tore his mouth away only long enough to whisper, "Spread your legs for me."

Without hesitating, she did as she was told. Her inhibitions seemed to be evaporating with Nick.

Was he going to fuck her right now?

After last night, she wouldn't put it past him, but at any moment, Lauren or Camille could walk in. They'd be scarred for life. She was about to protest, explain to him how this was not the time or place, but the words died on her lips when his fingers played over her.

He teased he vulva, the contact causing her to dampen. Last night she'd been so soaked, so wet that even this morning she found her panties still trying to cope with her body's response. Throughout the day, she'd managed to compose herself, but now Nick was at it again. It seemed, for her, dry panties were a thing of the past.

Nick inched lower, inserted his finger inside. Stopping, he pulled it out and proceeded to bathe her body with the moisture. He made several trips, each time pushing deeper inside her pussy, alternating between one and two fingers. Her body grabbed at him, trying to keep him deep inside. All the while, his thumb played rhythmically across her nipple, his tongue licking over hers.

Multiple sensations hit her, an orgasm was approaching

quickly. Dragging his fingers slowly over her clit, Nick removed his hand from her pants. She flinched at the withdrawal.

"No orgasm for you. You've been a bad girl," he taunted before holding up his wet fingers. "Open."

Timidly she obeyed, closing her lips around his fingers sucking off her own flavour. She cringed.

"You don't like that, eh?" He chuckled.

"Not particularly, no." *I'd rather taste you,* she thought.

"I think you taste delicious." Raising his hand, he licked off any remaining juices, before wiping his hand on his pants. He gave her breast a final squeeze before withdrawing from her body completely. Grabbing the washers that she'd dropped along with a ratty towel that was hanging near the door, he urged her to get a move on.

Stopping near the door, she turned to him. "Today's going to be hell, isn't it?"

His eyes sparkled. "For one of us it is." With that, he pushed back into the crisp winter air and called to the twins. "Girls, we found everything we needed in there."

* * * *

Nick was thoroughly enjoying himself. The day had been a complete success. Before Amelia had been called to help prepare dinner with Tammy and Sally, Nick had managed to catch her alone, twice. The first time she been on her way out of the hallway bathroom. He'd yanked her back inside and kissed her until they were both panting, and senseless. He'd forced her up onto the counter and dry humped her until he was painfully hard. Then he'd sent her on her way. It'd taken him a good five minutes to get himself back under control.

The second time he'd pinned her in the basement stairwell. Anthony and Gabe had been playing video games at the other end of the basement. Amelia had come down to get a drink from the bar for her grandfather and one for herself. With a beer in each hand, she was helpless to stop him. From behind, he'd rubbed against her. It hadn't taken long until she was pushing that lush ass against his groin.

He'd whispered some of the dirty thoughts that had occupied his mind all day. "Next time I get you alone you're going to get on your knees and I'm going to fuck that pretty little mouth of yours." When she groaned her agreement, he'd had to cough to cover up the sound.

Giving her ass a swat, he'd sent her on her way, but she'd turned on him. "I've spent two days dripping wet for you. I'm going to get even."

He'd laughed at her.

As the day grew later, Anthony was called up to help his sisters set the dinner table. Gabe downed the last of his beer. Grabbing up both the empties, Nick took them back to the bar. "You want another for dinner?"

"Nah," Gabe waved him off. "I'll probably have wine."

An awkward silence fell, which was rare for them. They'd had very few fights over the years, but Nick could tell something was wrong with Gabe today. Nick shrugged it off, he was probably reading too much into it. It was probably just a hangover.

"So I guess Cody got the message last night."

Nick popped the empty bottles back into the box. "I guess so."

"You've spent a lot of time with her today. Has she said anything?"

Maybe that was Gabe's problem. He was still smarting from Amelia's tongue-lashing last night. Yet, with Gabe watching him intently, Nick felt like this was some sort of trap. Leaning his hips against the bar, he thought over his answer. "No she hasn't said anything about it. But then things are still a little awkward, you know?"

"Is she still mad about what happened?" Gabe didn't need to elaborate. They both knew what incident he was referring to.

Trying not to sound too pained by the truth, Nick said, "I honestly don't know."

And he didn't. It was the one thing that was bothering him. What kind of relationship did they have? He knew he wanted her long term. He wanted to tell her family. He wanted to give them a try. But after what he did to her, was she willing to try again?

"Has she said anything to you?"

Pity flashed across Gabe's face. "About you or Cody?"

It was on the tip of his tongue to say either, but he feared that would give him away. "Cody. Obviously."

"No. She didn't say anything to me, but she still seems a little pissed at me for last night. I guess we're both in the same boat."

"And no oars in sight."

Gabe chuckled. Just then, Amelia hollered down at them, almost proving Gabe's point. "Dinner!"

Nick followed Gabe up the stairs. As they approached the dining room, they split up. Sally called Gabe in to help carry the wine bottles to the table. "Pour your grandfather a glass of red please."

"Nicholas!" Tammy waved him over, motioning to the empty chair between her and Amelia. "Come, sit here."

Tammy was making this so much easier for him. Taking the seat she offered, he poured her a glass of white wine while chatting with her. Purposely, he didn't say a word to Amelia, simply giving her a polite smile.

The dinner went smoothly, although he found Chris watching him, apparently taking in how he and Amelia were interacting. Besides the general conversation, and the passing of food, they ignored each other.

The food started circling the table a second time. Sally went to start the coffee machine. The conversation became livelier as the wine glasses were drained and some refilled.

When Nick had poured himself a half a glass more, Amelia asked him to top her off as well. Her cheeks were a little rosy as she reached for her glass. Nick wondered how many beers she'd had before dinner.

"I think last night was a huge success," Evelyn said from the other end of the table. "When will you know how much was raised?"

"We raised a few thousand off donations at the door. But we won't know how much the total is until the bar tab is tallied and all the donations counted," Sally replied.

Beside him, Amelia took a sip of her wine. Beneath the table, he felt her slip her hand from her knee to his.

"That's truly wonderful," Tammy said. "Not everyone is as blessed as us, I'm glad you've thought to give a little extra help to those who need it around Christmas."

Nick's pulse picked up as Amelia's fingers crept up his thigh. *This is so not the time or the place,* he thought as he willed his dick to stay down, but the damned thing wasn't interested in listening to him.

Anthony protested as Chris ruffled his hair. "Every kid should have a nice Christmas."

Thankful for the red tablecloth that draped his lap, Nick took a swallow of wine. He could feel her studying his face while her palm slid across his erection. Softly she rubbed him under the table, his dimensions growing in his jeans. He was so turned on, and so uncomfortable.

Lauren had been wearily pushing peas around on her plate. "Aunt Sally, what's for dessert?"

Sally was about to answer when Evelyn cut her off. "Not until you finish what's on your plate."

With a sneer, Lauren plucked a pea off the plate and plopped it in her mouth.

Amelia traced the outline of his dick through the denim, before finding and cupping his balls. Biting the inside of his cheeks, he straightened in his chair. The little nymph took another sip of wine. He wasn't sure if it was the booze that was making her bold, or if this was her attempt to get even with him for last night.

Tammy and Sally disappeared into the kitchen to start bringing in the desserts. Nick declined both pie and coffee. Not big on sugar Nick found it easy to turn down Tammy's pumpkin pie. But when Amelia also declined, her mother seemed a little confused.

"I'm just going to have more wine." She had to remove her hand from his lap to top up her glass again. "Ooh, and a cookie." While she was busy snagging a sugar cookie from the tray of goodies, Nick slipped his hand beneath the tablecloth to ward off her next attack.

Sure enough, she'd barely swallowed the cookie before her hand was creeping back up his thigh. He removed it and laced her fingers with his. She drew little circles back and forth on his palm, and he began to unwind. The second his fingers loosened, she jerked her hand away and made a beeline for his crotch again.

Any movement they made had to be subtle so as not to disturb the tablecloth. Nick chased down her hand and the battle for supremacy began. He'd much rather have them both naked some place where they could enjoy Amelia's sudden desire to molest him. Getting busted at the dinner table for a hand job was the last thing he wanted. So when dessert came to a close and Sally got up to clear the table, Nick jumped at the chance to escape.

"I'll give you a hand with the dishes."

Again Sally looked confused. Tammy seemed a little

disappointed, but Amelia was trying not to laugh. Nick grabbed up a few things off the table. Reaching for the basket of buns gave him an excuse to get close enough to whisper in her ear, "You're going to pay for that."

He felt her nipple tighten as he *accidently* bumped his arm against her breast. In response, she sent him a dirty look, giving him at least a little satisfaction.

Between Sally, Evelyn, Tammy and Nick the table was cleared quickly. Most of the dishes had been rinsed and tucked into the dishwasher, and the remaining ones had been washed, dried and put away.

"Here," Sally indicated toward the towel Nick had been using to dry. "Thanks for helping."

"No problem." He passed over the dishtowel and started to leave the kitchen, but changed his mind. "Thanks for everything."

Folding the towel, she looked puzzled. "What do you mean?"

"Well, what Chris was saying earlier about every kid deserving a good Christmas, if it wasn't for you guys always including me most of my childhood memories would have sucked. Despite my parents being major drunks, my life turned out alright, and I have you and Chris to thank for that."

Evelyn ducked out of the kitchen, leaving them to their moment, but Tammy hugged him.

He'd not only spent holidays with them, they'd invited him to stay when his parents had temporarily kicked him out, and a few times when he'd just had too much of their shit. It had been an ongoing joke that he was their extra child. But it was more than just a room at the Fuller's. Sally had helped him with his homework, especially those times when he'd struggled with math. And Chris had shown him how to work on cars and given him summer jobs whenever he needed extra money.

"I can't thank you enough."

Tammy sniffled, but released him.

Sally shook her head. "Nick, you've always been like part of the family. We're proud of how you turned out, what you've done with your life." She reached up and gave him a quick peck on the cheek. "You're a sweet kid."

Tammy and Sally headed back to the dining room.

The problem with open concept houses was privacy. When Nick turned around, he spotted Gabe and Amelia leaning on the island, both failing to hide their amusement. In sync with each other, they released a long, "Awww..."

"Oh shut up." But they both laughed.

"I've got to go pick up Paige."

Amelia perked up. "We'll go pick out a movie."

Nick nodded. Finally his chance to get her alone.

Gabe tossed on his coat and shoes, grabbed his keys and walked out the door.

"Cool! What movie? Can we come, too?" Anthony demanded. He and his sisters boxed Amelia in.

Halfway to the stairs, Nick paused. He and Amelia exchanged a heated look. After her foreplay at the table and their continued groping throughout the day, he needed her bad.

* * * *

"Hey," Evelyn called, "leave your cousins alone. They've played with you plenty today. You guys can watch a movie up here."

Amelia breathed a sigh of relief. Having young cousins was sometimes a pain in the ass. Aunt Evelyn no doubt assumed that any movie they'd want to watch would be inappropriate for her children to see, but based on the look

Nick just sent her, the movie wouldn't be the only thing unsuitable for them to witness.

Praying for no more interruptions, Amelia followed Nick down the stairs to the empty basement.

Waiting for Nick to make the first move, Amelia strode ahead of him into the living area. She picked a Christmas movie off the shelf and tossed it on the coffee table. "Alibi covered."

Nick pushed open the door to his room and, with a dark smile, beckoned for her to follow.

The little pot lights from the adjoining room cast limited light in his secluded space. She let out a small squeak when he made a grab for her as she entered the room.

"Finally," he muttered before his mouth closed over hers.

His fingers sank beneath her hair to curl around her nape. With his thumb, he pushed her jaw upward, holding her just as he wanted, opening her deeper for his kiss. Spinning slowly, he backed her into the room, never once allowing her mouth to leave his.

Her hands disappeared into his hair, pulling him closer. Eagerly, urgently they made out, devouring each other. When her back hit the wall, he took her hands from his hair and encouraged her to hold her arms above her head, and keep them there. Using the wall for balance, she did as she was told.

Nick tugged her t-shirt up over her breasts and dipped his hands inside her bra. Seconds later, he was kissing her, and it took everything she had to keep her hands above her head. It wasn't long before her muscles felt shaky from the odd position. Fortunately Nick pulled back to quickly strip her of her shirt and bra.

Naked from the waist up, he instructed her to stay, her arms still held high above her. She watched as he went to close the door. It was pitch dark. She could hear him shuffling around the room. Anticipation coursed through her.

He switched the bedside lamp on. It didn't give off as much light as the ceiling bulb, but the glow was intimate and romantic. Amelia's pulse kicked up a notch. He'd removed his shirt.

"Look at that! For once you actually did what you were told."

Heat flushed her cheeks. She said nothing. The wine from dinner mixed with the taste of Nick left her slightly dizzy.

Her gaze zeroed in on his hands as they began undoing his belt, then his jeans, then his fly. Her mouth watered when he removed his erection, stroking it as he came toward her.

"Perhaps you deserve a treat."

Amelia nodded.

"You want it?" he taunted.

Again she nodded.

Placing his palms on either side of her head, Nick leaned close and looked her in the eyes. "You can drop your arms now." Then he said the words she'd been waiting for. "In fact, you can drop all the way down to your knees."

"Yes." Amelia couldn't help the hiss that ripped from her throat as she descended.

She grasped the base and stroked him.

"No teasing. We're limited on time."

Glancing up, she caught his eye, licked her lips and whispered, "Yes, Sir."

Pinned between the wall and Nick's solid body, Amelia wet her lips, opened her mouth and drew him inside. She licked him from base to tip, swirled her tongue around the tip before taking him as deep as she could. Her gag reflex protested, but when she heard his long groan, she closed her eyes and fought it a little longer. When the tears began welling in the corner of her eyes, she eased off to a safer depth.

She held him with one hand and focused her attention on

the back and forth motion of her mouth. The saliva that built helped to make it easier for him to fuck her mouth. His precum collected at the end of his foreskin. She licked the bead of it away before taking just the tip to suck on.

Swallowing she started all over again. His panting increased.

Peeking up, Amelia studied Nick. His head hung low between his shoulders. His palms were flat on the wall, but his fingers had bent as he fought his control. His chest heaved and his abs quivered as she enjoyed her treat.

The way he was standing it was so easy to imagine him in the shower, the water hitting his back, and dripping down his chest onto her cheeks as she sucked him. She'd never showered with a man before and now she found herself wondering if she'd get the chance with Nick. She could imagine him holding her open before the shower, warm water cascading down her body, his fingers gliding in and out of her.

Exhaling through her nose, she tried not to focus on the growing need that was making her sex heavy.

Suddenly he opened his eyes. "You okay?"

Amelia pulled back and wiped her mouth, but never stopped stroking him. "Yes, Sir, but I'm not done yet."

Nick laughed. "I want you to go as deep as you can. Tap my knee if it's too much, or you want to stop."

"Okay."

"Open."

God, he excited her.

She did as she was told and took him as deep as she dared. After only a few strokes of her mouth, she felt his hand encase the back of her head, knotting in her hair. He guided her, quickening her pace.

It should have scared her, having no control, but it turned her on to know he was using her body as he wanted. Taking from her what he needed.

"Amelia," he breathed, "*yes.*"

Helpless, she moaned her pleasure. Unconsciously, she'd begun rolling her hips trying to ease her own cravings.

His dick hit the back of her throat. His pace increased. She breathed through her nose, her jaw was aching, but she knew he was close.

He groaned, gritted his teeth, and came. His hot seed shot down her throat. His hard dick pulsed under her tongue's attention. "*Amelia. Fuck, yes.*"

Her own body pulsed, begging for a release that still wasn't permitted for several hours. Slowly, he pulled back from her. Moments passed as they remained there, each catching their breath. He loomed over her. Shirtless, she rolled back onto her feet, her shoulders resting against the wall.

Her hands were still shaking when he lowered himself and clasped them. "You really are incredible."

It seemed he wanted to say something more. Amelia waited, but when he refused to speak his mind, she just smiled, acting as though it didn't matter that they still hadn't shared any deep feelings.

He pressed a kiss to her forehead before passing her discarded bra and shirt back to her. She hurried to pull them on as he took a few minutes to compose himself.

Pretending that what they'd done didn't mean more to her than just sex, she headed for the door. "Can you pop the DVD in? I'll go make some popcorn."

Nick's eyes narrowed. She wasn't sure if it was the order she'd dictated to him, or the fact that she was rushing out on him, but either way he made no move to stop her.

For reasons she didn't quite understand, she found herself fighting tears as she made her way through the basement and up the stairs.

Trotting around the living room, Amelia glanced at her cousins watching *Elf* on *Netflix.* Ironic since that's what lay on the table downstairs.

"Amelia, your cheeks are really red," her mother noted with disapproval as she came gliding into the dining room.

"I'm fine." Amelia retrieved her wine glass and took a long sip, washing away the salty after taste of Nick's release.

In the kitchen, she set about making popcorn. While the kernels started to heat, she collected the butter and the salt. Her dad followed her into the kitchen. Leaning against the counter, he studied her. "How much have you had to drink today?"

"One beer and a couple of glasses of wine. Really, Dad, I'm fine."

"Gabe mentioned you had a lot to drink last night."

Amelia scowled. Now they were gossiping about her? "Gabe doesn't know what he's talking about."

The air popper got louder. Her dad lowered his voice, but she could still hear him when he asked, "Whose idea was it to keep it a secret?"

Not bothering to pretend she didn't understand, she blurted out, "Mine."

He scrutinized her. "Whose idea was it really?"

Amelia exploded. "Mine, alright? God!" Then a second thought hit her. "You didn't tell anyone, did you? Mom?" She gasped. "Grandma?"

"No. Are you kidding me? The second your grandmother finds out everyone will know. No, I haven't told anyone. It's just," he hesitated, "are you sure about this?"

"Why are you so ready to paint him as the bad guy?"

Her dad threw his hands up in the air. "I'm not. I like Nick. He's a great guy. But..."

"Dad, don't worry about me. I know what I'm doing." *Sort of.*

"You're my daughter, I'm always going to worry."

She gave him a kiss on the cheek. "That's sweet, Dad, but don't worry. I got this." She offered him a handful of popcorn before taking the first batch in to her younger cousins. Her dad stayed in the kitchen and chatted with her about school until she'd finished making two more bowlfuls.

By the time she'd finished putting the toppings on, Gabe and Paige were back. She passed Paige one of the bowls. Going back to the dining room where the adults were still gathered, Amelia grabbed the half bottle of white wine on the table. Tucking it under one arm, she grabbed up her glass in one hand and the popcorn bowl in the other.

When they made it downstairs, Nick was seated on the end of one of the couches. The basement was dark except the title screen that lit up the room.

Paige sunk into the couch opposite from Nick. Gabe sat with her. While Nick hit play on the remote, Amelia settled in next to him. The opening credits panned across the screen as the story started, but Amelia's mind had begun to wander.

Really what was she doing with Nick? He pushed for exclusiveness. He didn't seem to mind when others found out about them. He was taking an interest in her Dom/sub fantasy, and the way he talked seemed to indicate some sort of future. But what?

Was this just sexual? Would it end when she went back to school? Was he just amusing himself for a few weeks?

She didn't think so. But she'd been wrong before.

She was so aware of him as he sat silently beside her, watching the movie. Occasionally he'd reach for popcorn. She found herself wanting to lick the butter off his fingers, which only brought her thoughts back to that afternoon in the garage.

He twirled a strand of hair around his finger. If it was just sex he wouldn't be playing with her hair. Unless she'd picked a boring movie.

Emotionally and sexually frustrated, Amelia found that no matter how she looked at it, it all came back to the same question. What the hell had changed in the last three years?

Chapter Thirteen

Something weird was going on and Gabe didn't like it, not one bit. He couldn't quite put his finger on it. Often times when their grandparents came to visit, his grandmother made comments constantly about Nick and Amelia, trying, much to everyone's dismay to get them together. But this trip she'd been uncharacteristically quiet on the subject.

Generally Nick avoided Amelia whenever he could, but today he'd spent more time around the house, playing with Camille, Lauren, and Amelia rather than going snowmobiling with the guys. Maybe he was nursing a hangover, much like Gabe was. Or maybe he was simply being extra nice to Amelia so she wouldn't disappear at school again.

Whatever the reason, there was something different. After last night's fight with Amelia there was very little he could say. She didn't want him involved and that was that. At least that rat Cody had disappeared. As far as he knew, Cody hadn't tried to contact Amelia today. Gabe supposed he'd gotten the message. He'd threatened to have Cody thrown out of the party if he even attempted to approach Amelia again.

Today, something different prickled him. When his family had been called to dinner, Gabe found himself with a new problem. Nick had seated himself beside Amelia. Sure, Grandma was on his other side and he'd smiled and chatted to her while he took his seat, but it just didn't sit well with Gabe.

Once dinner came to an end, Gabe was scheduled to go

pick up Paige.

"We'll go pick out a movie," Amelia had said cheerfully. Nick nodded his agreement a little too quickly.

Gabe had grumbled to himself all the way to the car. He'd been tempted to accompany them to the basement and forget Paige, but his grandma would put him through the ringer again if he tried to ditch his boyfriend responsibilities.

This sham of a relationship with Paige was beginning to grate on his nerves. They'd been dating for nearly four months now, surely that was long enough to appease his mother. Once they were safely through the holidays, he decided it would be time to end things. Paige would be relieved to hear his plan.

Currently, Paige sat curled under his arm as they all watched *Elf.* For his part, Gabe found himself watching Nick interact with his sister, almost as much as he paid attention to the movie.

It didn't go unnoticed that Nick had chosen to sit beside Amelia on the couch. Sure, they were sharing a bowl of popcorn, same as he and Paige were, but Gabe didn't like it one bit that Nick had to reach into the bowl that sat smack dab in the middle of Amelia's crossed legs.

At one point Nick had stretched his arm along the back of the sofa, and Gabe was sure he saw his best friend playing with a strand of Amelia's hair.

Nick's words from last night came back to haunt him. *Who I fuck, and where I fuck is none of your business.*

Nick looked over then and was caught in his glare. Picking up on Gabe's unease, Nick's eyes narrowed in response. His arm remained anchored to the back of the couch.

I'm on to you, Gabe thought. Paige dipped her hand into the popcorn bowl, giving him the necessary distraction to avert his gaze back to the screen.

* * * *

Cradling his head in his hands Nick reclined on his bed, waiting for Amelia to come downstairs. Naked, he was anxious to get started. He'd left the heavy duvet at the end of the bed along with the winter blankets, leaving only the fleece sheet covering his lower body.

After the movie ended, they'd played cards. Paige and Amelia had teamed up opposite him and Gabe for a game of euchre. He and Gabe had sucked, they'd barely taken four points between them, and as partners they'd come through for each other maybe once. Nick didn't know what the hell had gotten into his friend, but it seemed like he was intentionally screwing them over. Paige had picked up on Gabe's hostility and tried to reach out to him. He'd snapped at her. They didn't stick around long after the game was over.

A soft knock drew him out of his thoughts. "Come in."

Amelia closed the door behind her.

"You shut off the rest of the basement lights?"

"Yeah."

"Good." He didn't want Gabe to think they were still up. He interrupted them far too often.

Nick didn't bother getting up from the bed. "Come here."

The soft glow of the lamp illuminated her as she came toward him. Standing next to the bed, she seemed to hesitate with uncertainly. "Part the robe."

The satin tie slithered when she tugged it free. The royal blue sea split leaving her bare down the middle. The curves of her breasts were visible, her tight tummy, the dark curls above the apex of her thighs. She'd changed her belly button ring and replaced it with one that resembled a snowflake.

Clutching the edge of the robe, he pulled her down toward the bed. Willingly, she climbed onto the mattress and straddled him.

With one knee on each side of his hips, she hovered over

him, running her palms up and down his chest. Her focus seemed to be somewhere else, her thoughts wandering as she stared down at him.

Lightly, he touched her cheek. She didn't smile, her normal cheerfulness was absent. "Are you alright?"

His words must have brought her out of her musing. This time when she looked at him, he could see the doubt in her eyes. He wondered if he'd taken this whole Dom/sub thing too far. Was she still enjoying it? She'd been an eager participant all day. Not once had he forced her to do anything she didn't want to. At dinner, she'd initiated their play. And last night, she'd been as ecstatic as he was when he'd taken her in that bathroom.

Yes, she wanted this. So where had the spirited woman from dinner disappeared to?

She nodded. About to push her for an honest answer, she distracted him with a roll of her hips. Her sex pushed against his forcing matching moans from them. The emotion in her gaze changed to something heated, something sexual, and his body responded.

Slipping the robe off her shoulders, he let his hands linger rubbing over her arms. Naked and straddling him her body was completely exposed, her legs splayed, and her breasts heavy. She took his breath away.

* * * *

Shyly, Amelia peeked at Nick from beneath her lashes. His fingers glided over her arms, teasing the soft skin of her elbows before floating over to brush her breasts. Playing, he ground his palm against her flesh. Her nipples responded, tightening under his attention.

Desperately she wanted to understand what Nick really thought of her, of what was going on between them, besides the hot sex. Terrified, in her mind she'd gone over all the possible ways to broach the subject with him, but sitting naked astride him, she thrust the thoughts out of her mind.

She'd read the concern on his face. She'd wait, keep her mouth shut and enjoy him and his wonderful body. His skin was warm beneath her touch. Her body answered every movement his body made, every command he whispered. Since losing her virginity at seventeen, sex had always been just a thing, something to do, to get off quickly and move onto the next thing. But with Nick she cherished all of it, she was giddy and anxious each time she thought of him. Did she really want to put that at risk after only a week?

"Kiss me," he demanded, using her erect nipples simultaneously to tug her closer. She went willingly, lightly pressing her lips to his. Soon their kisses turned more persistent. Amelia raised her body when he reached down to remove the sheet that separated them. His searching fingers slid through her slick folds. Flirting with her entrance, he teased her, their locked lips never parting.

She squirmed as his touch continued to excite her. Breaking their kiss for some much-needed air, Amelia buried her nose in his neck, inhaling his unique scent.

"What time is it?" he asked, rolling over to grab a condom.

The clock read ten to twelve. She gave him the time, but silently wondered why it mattered.

"Ten minutes before you're allowed to come. You have to hold off any orgasms."

Against his throat, she groaned. His chest rose and fell with his laugh. The second he stopped, his demeanour changed. Quietly, he said, "Ride me."

Her muscles clenched with the softly spoken, erotic command. Bracing herself with one hand, she grasped his cock with the other. Gradually she lowered herself. Her body widened to accommodate his size. Inch by inch he entered her, and when at last she was filled, he yanked her back to him.

Chest to chest they lay together, appreciating their joined bodies. At length, Amelia began to move. With her hands on his pillow, she dragged her body upward toward the head of the bed, only to sink back down. They groaned in unison. She did it again, working her thigh muscles, moving her hips, her breasts heaving against him. Each movement shook her to the core. Her clitoris rubbed against his pubic hair, pleasuring her outside, each stroke of his cock creating the same sensation inside. The dual stimulation rocked her.

His big hand clamped down on her ass. "Don't come yet."

Beneath her curled toes, she felt his calf muscles clench. He was close, too, fighting off the release that would end this sweet torment. Using her arms, she pushed her body upward to ride him in earnest.

"Did I tell you, you could sit up?"

She practically fell back toward the mattress.

"That's a good girl."

Holy fuck! She never thought being treated like a possession would get her so hot, but at his heated words, she felt a mini orgasm rake her body.

Bracing herself on her elbows, she worked his cock, keeping the slow rhythm that had her panting. He was right, this position kept him deep, the way she rocked on her hands and knees kept them both on the ragged edge.

Restraint fraying, her muscles protested at the unfamiliar workout. Her triceps quivered from fatigue, her thighs began to ache from being stretched over him. Her whole body shook from the extended pleasure. She was turned on by the sound of her own strained breath.

His hands circled her hips before dipping down her backside. With one hand on each cheek, his fingers spanned her ass. She shivered. He kissed her shoulder, his lips lingering, his tongue stroking her flesh. Her vaginal muscles started to convulse, she tried to stop it. Tears welled in her eyes, but it was useless. "I can't stop it."

So focused she barely noticed as he turned his head to check the clock. "Twelve o' two," he whispered.

Relief rushed through her, freeing the last limitations on her climax. Unable to control herself, she bit his shoulder, stifling her cries as her body gripped him, her cream coating him even more. "That's right, baby." His hands clenched on her buttocks while he continued to rock her body, urging her on. "Give it to me, all of it."

Nick clenched beneath her. She felt him go from hard to steel inside her as he pulsed his release. Her orgasm rode her hard. Together they collapsed.

He didn't force her off, instead he lay sheathed by her body. Tears spilled from her eyes, the power of her orgasm ruining her emotional control. The last thing she wanted was to explain herself to Nick. Turning her head, she wiped her eyes on his pillow praying he didn't notice.

His heartbeat pounded against her chest. He petted her hair.

In the aftermath of their intimacy, Amelia had no choice but to face the harsh reality. She was still in love with Nick. In three years, for her, nothing had changed. Now all that was left was for everyone to discover how big a fool she really was.

Chapter Fourteen

Each year on Christmas Eve it was tradition for the kids to open one present. Sally and Chris started it years ago when Gabe and Amelia were young. On Christmas Eve, they would open their Christmas pajamas and one gift addressed to the family. It was always a board game that was immediately opened and enjoyed over hot cocoa. More than twenty years later the tradition was not only continued, but expanded to include the extended family.

Nick, Gabe and Amelia all sat in brand new pajamas watching as Camille and Lauren, in matching onesies, tore at one end of a long box wrapped in snowman print. Anthony pushed back the sleeves of his new bathrobe in order to get a better grip on his end of the box. The adults laughed as the kids struggled to open the package. Aunt Evelyn had a nasty habit of using too much tape.

When they had finally succeeded, Anthony ran around the room with a trash bag to collect all the discarded wrapping paper. He knew his Aunt Sally wouldn't let them play until everything was tidy, although Amelia suspected he was just as excited to get his mint hot cocoa. While Anthony raced to clean up, the girls began opening the game to unwrap its components.

Nick leaned forward from his spot on a folding chair to whisper in Camille's ear. The little girl's eyes lit up. She pushed up from the floor and rushed to the Christmas tree.

Amelia's heart began to thud as Camille came barreling toward her with the thin rectangular box that Nick had left for her beneath the tree.

Sally, who was about to get up to make the cocoa, stopped halfway and reseated herself. Amelia felt the eyes of all the adults and realized she wasn't the only one curious about the contents of the box. She couldn't bring herself to look at Nick, even though she felt his eyes burning into her.

When he'd warned her not to let anyone see the engraving, she'd planned to open it in private. Now he had taken that option away from her, it was probably a deliberate move on his part, to make her uncomfortable. To make her sweat.

Her mom was intent on seeing whatever Nick had placed in the box. Amelia prayed the engraving was hidden. The envelope that housed the card was plain white. Scribbled across the front he'd written who it was for and who it was from. She licked her dry lips and bravely opened the little card that accompanied the package.

Don't worry. I got you a real one, too.

– Nick

Placing the card back into the envelope Amelia tried for nonchalance as she tucked it between her thigh and the couch cushion. She didn't know how she'd explain such a message if her family made her read it out loud.

The twins had nearly finished unpacking the game.

Sandwiched between her mother and the arm of the couch, Amelia struggled to keep her fingers from shaking as she tugged off the ribbon. Flipping open the lid, she peeked inside.

"Oh, that's pretty," her mother cooed.

A dainty sterling silver anklet was tucked inside. Opposite the clasp, in the centre of the chain was a heart. Amelia sunk into the couch with relief. The engraving had to be on the other side of the heart. *Thank god!*

The second her mother glanced away, Amelia flipped the heart over. The engraving was his initials. *N.K.*

She tossed his scribbled words over in her mind. A real

one. One what?

Her gaze flew to Nick as comprehension sank in. Like an animal tracking its prey, his stare never wavered from her. She tried to keep her breath from accelerating, but it was a struggle, almost as though she could feel the imagined material constricting around her neck.

It was a collar.

Her mother nudged her. "Well thank him."

The corner of Nick's mouth twitched as her mother reminded of her manners.

Amelia pasted on her most fake smile. If she was to be coerced into submitting to his control, she'd fight it with kindness. "Yes, thank you, Nick. This was very *sweet* of you."

"You're welcome." Amelia wondered if anyone else could detect the undertone of mastery that resided in his words.

Amelia put the lid back on the box. "So, let's try out this new game!"

"Amelia!" Her grandmother scolded, "Don't be rude. Put it on."

Across the room, Nick placed two fingers over his lips to suppress his laughter. Putting on the anklet held so much more meaning than her grandmother would ever know, would ever be able to comprehend. If she put it on, it symbolized his ownership of her. She wasn't sure that she was ready for such a big step.

"Later, Grandma."

The Fullers were not a democracy. They were led by a matriarch, and Amelia now found herself on the wrong side of that matriarch.

"It looks to me like Nick spent good money on that trinket. Show him your appreciation. Put it on."

Amelia clenched her teeth and opened the box once more. Stalling, she pushed the chain around on the cotton batten, until Anthony cut into her thoughts. "Come on, Amelia. Put it on so we can play."

Kids and their one-track minds! Shaking her head at Anthony, she pulled the anklet out of its home. She forced herself to watch Nick's face as she leaned down and fastened the jewellery to her body. There was a hint of laughter in his eyes, but it was mixed with something else, something powerful. Possession.

She tingled with the pressing need to feel his touch. Suddenly she couldn't wait to be alone with him, and the weight of the anklet reminded her that it was only a matter of time.

* * * *

Gabe was going to kill him.

Nick had never been so thankful for Gabe having a religious girlfriend. Shortly after the kids started playing their new board game, Gabe had to leave for the candle lit Christmas Eve service at Paige's church. Dating the pastor's daughter made his attendance mandatory. It bought Nick at least a day before he had to deal with Gabe's rage.

His relationship with Amelia was out of the bag now. Everyone knew he'd bought her jewellery. It was significant, no doubting that, but now each member of the Fuller family was left wondering exactly what it meant. But Gabe *knew.*

He'd felt Gabe's anger from the second she opened the box. It had taken all his strength to keep from looking over at his friend in those moments. If he'd looked, it would have been like signing a confession. Sooner or later, he'd have to deal with Gabe, but for now, he wanted to focus his attention on Amelia.

She hadn't wanted to put the anklet on. It had pleased him when she'd put the lid on the box like a flat out refusal to submit. It had pleased him even more when Tammy had demanded she put it on.

All night he'd bided his time. When Tammy had prompted him to join in for a round of the new board game, he'd played with enthusiasm and helped Anthony to win. He'd had a beer with Chris, Jacob and George while they talked over the hockey prospects for the winter season. The kids fought with Evelyn over their bedtime, and succeeded in winning an extra hour before Sally and Evelyn read *The Night before Christmas* and put them to bed.

Not long after, Nick wished everyone a Merry Christmas and headed downstairs. He wasn't particularly keen on the idea of being upstairs when Gabe got home. Nick watched a Christmas flick on his phone while he waited for everyone to go to bed. Occasionally he sent Amelia a few text messages to heighten her anticipation for the night he had planned.

He listened for the sounds of the household falling asleep. Laughter lessened, the hum of conversation slowed. The stairs groaned as people ascended to their rooms. Running water signified the brushing of teeth, toilets flushing in succession indicated that multiple people were preparing to crawl between the sheets.

Half an hour later, he pulled a bag out of the dresser and checked its contents to make sure everything was in order for tonight's session. There were no bedside tables in the guest bedroom, so he placed the bag on the shelving that fit the headboard. Then he sent Amelia a text, *Play Time.*

* * * *

Amelia knocked softly on the French style doors. When Nick opened them, she couldn't hold her tongue. "You're a bastard, you know."

He leaned in the doorway and leered at her, his smug, lazy smile distracting her from her anger.

"That was a nasty trick and you know it."

"And you just love to break the rules." He did a slow perusal of her outfit.

Not changing out of her flannel pajamas had been a deliberate decision. "You humiliated me. You set me up."

He ignored her. "If you don't follow the rules then I can't give you what you want."

"And you know what I want?" She crossed her arms over her chest.

"Yes." Still hanging in the doorframe, he leaned closer and murmured as though he were telling her a secret, "You're angry because you're horny."

She huffed.

He scratched the scruff that had accumulated on his jaw throughout the day. "Your nipples are tight. I can see them even through the flannel. Your pupils are dilated. Your back is arched. You want to come."

He had her there. All night she'd felt the anklet against her skin sending shivers up her body. Nick grabbed her hand and dragged it to his crotch. "And you want this," he finished as he wrapped her hand around his engorged cock. She stroked him through the cotton of his pajama bottoms until he stopped her. "Get in here."

Nick shut the door behind her. "Show it to me."

The mattress dipped as Amelia sat on the edge of the bed and lifted her pant leg to reveal the silver anklet. His gaze swept over her. "Your grandma really loves me." He grinned. "Take off your clothes. I want to see you in just the anklet."

Amelia resisted. Nick waited. Nick won.

Impatience got the best of her and she began unbuttoning her shirt, starting at the collar.

"Bottoms first."

Amelia rolled her eyes. She was convinced he was trying to be an ass. Standing up, she loosened the drawstring and shimmied out of the bottoms. They dropped to the floor, but she left them were they fell, binding her ankles, but hiding the jewellery. Leaving her panties on, she started again with the buttons, this time she slipped the ones at the base of the shirt free to leave her breasts covered until the very end.

When all the buttons were undone, she slipped the shirt off her shoulders and cast it to the floor. Immediately her nipples puckered in the cold air. She stubbornly raised her chin and drew off her panties. She kicked them and the pajamas away.

Nick pulled himself away from the door to inspect her. He crouched before her and spun the anklet around and around before looking up. "Very nice."

His face was inches from her. Her fingers itched to pull him to her, to insist he place urgent kisses to her mound, to lick her until she came. But she dared not touch him. She didn't have permission.

His smile told her he knew what she was thinking. "Kneel on the bed, put your hands behind your head and link your fingers together."

Amelia scrambled to do just that. The position left her exposed. In order to keep her balance, she had to splay her knees shoulder width apart. When she raised her hands up, her breasts jutted out. She burned for his touch.

Nick palmed her right breast, moulding the weight, hefting it up before his long fingers traced her tight nipple. He pinched it hard, ripping a moan from her lips, and sending shockwaves straight to her sex. "You understand what the anklet is?"

"Yes."

"What is it?"

Of course he was going to make her say the words. "It's a collar."

He placed a wet kiss on her nipple before moving his attention to the other breast. "What does it mean?" Her lashes fluttered closed as she enjoyed the insistent tug of his mouth. When she didn't answer, he stopped. "What does it mean, Amelia?"

She flicked her eyelids open to look at him. "It means I'm yours. You own me."

Twice he stroked her cheek before he kissed her. Just a light peck before he went to the head of the bed to retrieve a bag. "I want you to wear the anklet all the time. It signifies that you belong to me. But this," he said, reaching into the bag, "is just for us."

Hanging from his hand was the collar.

It wasn't anything like she'd imagined. She'd been thinking black leather, maybe with some studs, or even a black frilly lace collar. Never would she have thought of this.

Her gaze swung from the collar to his face, and dumbly she muttered, "That's a dog collar."

"Yes."

"No, like that's an actual dog collar."

And it was. The collar was burnt orange. The locking mechanism and all the other hardware had a gunmetal-finish. One portion had the manufacturer's logo on it. There was a loop attached for a leash.

Amelia looked back at the bag. She'd bet money there was a leash in there. He held the collar toward her. "Put it on."

She almost rejected it, after all, it was a dog collar, but the safe word lodged in her throat. She trusted Nick to take her on this sexual journey. Taking the collar from him, she unlocked it, slipped it on, and fastened it. It gaped around her neck.

The mattress shifted as Nick leaned toward her to adjust it. As it tightened, the rough material chafed her soft skin. He edged closer to loosen it, until it hugged her in the perfect fit.

His bare skin rubbed against her tight nipples. She shifted, hoping to ease the burning need for his touch. He dragged his fingers through her hair. Gently he pulled her head back and ducked his face toward her neck. His tongue traced a line between the collar and her flesh, leaving her skin damp. He placed one open-mouthed kiss after another leading a path from the collar to her ear. "You're mine now. My perfect, little pet."

She groaned. He trailed his fingers down her back, traced the curve of her ass before giving it a playful swat.

Suddenly he was gone. She blinked at him as he fished through the bag once more to reveal a leash of matching orange. "You didn't arrive in the agreed upon attire. You should be punished, don't you agree? Hands and knees."

Amelia dropped to the requested position. There was no point in arguing with him. She had disobeyed, and squabbling would only increase the punishment, and delay things further. Despite everything she'd said, he was right. She wanted to get laid. She wanted it hard and rough, wanted to feel him buried deep inside her. Her muscles ached with the need to clamp around him. She suspected he wanted the same so she answered, "Yes."

He circled her, wrapping the leash around and around his palm. "Five lashes for your deliberate disobedience. You will count them out for me."

She'd never gone this far before. She was scared, but regardless, her body reached for him. She couldn't help but offer up her ass for his strikes. His hand loosened on the leash. It uncoiled, and taking the metal clasp in his hand, he allowed the nylon to dangle from his grip.

"Face forward, Amelia, and count."

Facing the wall she waited, just as she had the night they'd played ping-pong. And just as he had that night with the paddle, he let the anticipation build. She tried not to move. She didn't arch her back, or lean toward him.

Slap. The first lash fell.

"One." *Slap.* "Two." *Slap.* "Three."

Tears burned at the back of her eyes. *Slap.*

"Four."

The pain was so acute. The paddle had stung, but the leash was piercing. *Slap.*

"Five."

The leash fell again, this time the blow landing on the back of her thighs.

"You said five," she snapped, her head whipping to look over her shoulder.

Calmly he replied, "Are you questioning me?"

Amelia bit her lip and glanced at the ceiling. *Why couldn't she keep her mouth shut?*

"No," she lied.

He dragged the nylon across her reddening bottom. "Two additional lashes for your most recent insubordination." He pressed the leash against her clit, rubbing it upward with two firm fingers. The friction made her burn. "We'll start from the beginning." Leaning over her, his hard erection pressed against her sensitized flesh. His tongue flicked against her ear. "You get five more for calling me a bastard when you showed up here."

She moaned and writhed against him. The dual phenomenon of his dick against her ass and the rough leash against her clitoris had her rocking for release.

"Be still."

She nearly wept as she obeyed. *Who knew that stillness could be so painful?*

He removed the leash and replaced it with his fingers. He massaged her body, spreading her cream around, moistening her. His fingers circled her entrance. Her nails dug into the mattress as she fought not to move, not to scream.

"What should you have called me?"

If she answered right, he might press his fingers inside. She responded with, "Sir."

The tip of his finger wiggled in, just barely before pulling out. "Try again."

His finger made her more sensitive with each rotation as it continued its slow circular assault on her hole. With the leash hanging from his wrist, he looped his pinky through the attachment on the collar. Giving her a clue, he pulled on it. "You said, *you're a bastard, you know.* Is that any way to greet me? Tell me, Amelia, what should you have called me?"

Because her body demanded a smashing climax and only Nick could give it to her, she gathered her courage, and whispered the word that would lock her to him, "Master."

His fingers plunged into her. He rotated them, pushed deeper until he found her G-spot. Her hips bucked. He withdrew, and she had to grind her teeth to keep from crying out.

"Five for your attire. Five for the bastard comment. Two for insubordination. Count them out."

"Yes, Master." The first one landed on her ass. "Seven."

His laugh echoed behind her. "Try again."

"One."

From there he landed another eleven blows on her ass and thighs, the sharp sound of each strike rippled off the walls, and vibrated down her body to her core.

"Twelve," she finished, tears stinging her eyes. The leash struck her once more, but by now, she'd learned her lesson and hoarsely whispered, "Thirteen."

"Much better." The bed shifted as Nick rose up behind her. "Be still."

Something cold and hard touched her back. Goosebumps shot down her arms, across her chest the flesh rising, her nipples puckering even tighter, almost painfully. Nick dragged the metal attachment of the leash down the line of her spine. She tried not to bow her back against the cold assault on her skin.

Again and again he lowered the metal, flirting with her bare back, drawing imaginary lines across her shoulder blades, her hips, her back. He traced the dips of her body. Amelia had never realized how sensitive her back was, an area that was rarely naked, was rarely viewed by others, but now Nick laboured to give it equal attention.

At last, he replaced the metal with his own hands, first warming her skin, touching her everywhere. He smoothed his hand down her back and over the cheeks of her ass, calming the skin that still smarted from her punishment. His fingers eased over her and lightly massaged her shoulders, her neck, and her body.

He clicked the leash into place with the collar, joining the two toys. "Amelia, tell me that you're ready."

"Yes, Master. I'm ready. I'm so wet, I want—" her train of thought broke off as his big hands grasped her hips. His cock slid against her swollen pussy. Her body automatically gripped at nothing, wanting to be filled.

She hadn't exaggerated her dampness. He positioned himself at her entrance and slipped easily inside. They groaned in unison as they finally gave in to what they were craving. Amelia's arms shook from holding her up for such a long time, but when Nick began pumping into her body from behind, his grip firm and sure on her hips, she forgot all about the strain in her muscles, her entire being focused on the point where their bodies met. She rocked with him, her reddened butt scraping against his course pubic hair, tingling along her senses.

His pace increased, and Amelia knew he wouldn't last long. He was demanding, pushing her along with him. Sweat broke out across her body. The sound of her ass slapping against him pounded in her ears. Reaching around her, Nick's fingers fluttered over her clitoris. His other hand grabbed for the leash, but in their haste, it flung about, evading him.

Instead, he settled for a fist full of her hair, pulling her head back, and exciting her terribly.

His breath was hot in her ear as he laid light kisses against her throat. His fingers rubbed at her sensitive flesh. She hovered so close to the edge.

He traced the collar with his tongue, before his lips wrapped around the shell of her ear, "You're my proper little bitch now, aren't you?"

She went crashing. She couldn't stop from crying out as her body convulsed around him, trying to milk an orgasm from him. He held tight to his restraint.

He wouldn't let her recover, instead he stayed a constant growling into her ear, "Say it, Amelia. Say it."

"I'm your bitch. I'm your filthy little slut." And just that fast, he sent her tumbling over the cliff again. She dropped to her forearms, stifling her scream in his pillow as he slammed into her from behind, again and again until he shot his cum deep within her. Tears trekked down her face, her dual orgasms overwhelming her emotions.

They collapsed together, empty and spent onto the bed, their breathing laboured as pleasure racked their bodies. Nick draped his arm over her. "Come here."

Cuddling into his body Amelia combated with the knowledge that for the second time they'd forgotten the damn condom.

Chapter Fifteen

Nick loved the Fuller's family Christmases. He was beyond grateful that each year they let him join in their festivities. Being included in the Fuller family gatherings throughout the years helped him to forget what a fuck factory his own family was. As soon as he turned sixteen, he'd hightailed it out of his home, struggled his way through the rest of high school, and somehow made it through college. He might not have the most prestigious job but he was good at it and made more than he needed to support himself. After Fuller Homes and Construction was through building his home, Nick planned to take some more business management classes online, and maybe one day he'd be able to start his own personal fitness training company. If it wasn't for the Fullers, he'd never have made it out of the gutter.

As embedded as he was in the Fuller family, he couldn't resist when Camille and Lauren begged him to play Candyland with them. The girls were a little too old for the game, but traditions where important in the Fuller house, so Nick let himself be persuaded to play.

The girls sat side by side on the sofa, while Nick lounged on the floor. Tammy sat knitting in the corner and George had disappeared to take a nap. Camille was nearing the end of the board, when the front door opened and Gabe, Anthony and Chris came in wiping the snow from their boots and hair before removing their winter clothes. They'd spent the afternoon sledding.

"I think you girls are cheating." Nick scowled at them.

They giggled.

Gabe plopped down on the opposing couch and nodded at Nick. "They always cheat at Candyland."

Nick had been sure that Gabe was going to confront him about his extravagant gift. He'd glared daggers Nick's way ever since Christmas Eve, but with all the activities, they hadn't had a chance to talk. Today, Gabe had seemed in a better mood before he left with Paige to hit the Boxing Day Sales. He'd barely had time to put his parcels away before Anthony had been climbing all over him to go sledding. The tension had eased away from Nick. Maybe he'd luck out and not have to explain a damn thing to Gabe.

The aroma of freshly baked cookies started to fill the room as Amelia sashayed her way into the living room. She dropped onto the couch with Gabe. Hugging her knees, she propped her feet against her butt and cuddled into the cushions.

"Baking sure can take it out of you." She'd been baking all day with her mom and grandmother, until Tammy had complained her arthritis was getting too bad to stand. Amelia and Sally had finished up. She kicked her brother. "Apple pie for dessert tonight though."

"Grandma's recipe?" Gabe grabbed hold of her foot. Amelia squirmed.

"Of course." Tammy smiled at the warm room filled with her grandchildren.

Gabe tickled the bottom of Amelia's foot until she squealed. "Let go!"

When she retaliated by kicking at him with the other foot Gabe grabbed hold of that ankle as well. His grip changed. Gone was the playful mood, as he gripped her in an unyielding touch.

Nick tensed.

"Hey, let go." Amelia's tone held a warning note, but Gabe

merely grinned.

His fingers felt around her calves, until they came upon what he was looking for. He released her left ankle, and drew back her right pant leg. "I just want to have a look at the pretty anklet Nick gave you."

Nick felt Amelia's gaze fly to him. Panic welled within him, but he forced his attention back to the girls. "Whose roll is it? Lauren?"

The little blonde bobbed her head, scooted to the edge of the couch and grabbed for the die. While she rocked the die within her tiny clasped hands, Nick snuck a peek back at Gabe, awaiting his fate.

Gabe twirled the chain until he came up on the heart. He fingered it for a moment, flipping it over and over. His jaw worked in sync with his fingers. It seemed like forever that they waited as Gabe chewed over the anklet.

"I rolled a six!" Lauren shouted before moving her piece around the board. Her outburst seemed to break the tension.

Sucking in a breath, Gabe dropped Amelia's leg. "Nick, can I talk to you for a minute?"

Feigning innocence, Nick refused to move. "Sure. What's up?"

Gabe thrust up from the couch. "Privately."

Nick pursed his lips, his heart pounded fiercely in his chest. He knew this moment would come eventually, but he still didn't have anything prepared. Nothing he could say would ease Gabe's mind.

Nick pushed himself up. "Girls, can you excuse me for a minute? Maybe Amelia knows when those cookies will be ready."

He hoped to distract Amelia. The last thing he needed was her running after them to try and rescue him from her brother.

He followed Gabe down the steps to the basement. Nick braced himself for an attack, but none came.

Barely two feet away Gabe stood, hands on hips and glared at Nick as a deep silence settled over the basement. Gabe had never been particularly patient. He broke first. "Well, what do you have to say for yourself?"

Really, what could he say? Nick shrugged.

That's when Gabe lunged at him. "Goddamn it!" he yelled as he slammed Nick against the wall concealing the stairs.

"I'm not going to fight with you about this." Nick's voice bespoke a calm he didn't feel. Using his forearms, he blocked Gabe, keeping him from going for the jugular.

"It was her, wasn't it?"

"What are you talking about?"

Gabe drew him forward to shove him into the wall again. "In the bathroom. At the party. It was her, wasn't it?" When Nick remained silent, Gabe adjusted the grip on the front of his shirt. Any second now he was sure he'd feel Gabe's fist connect with his face, and he didn't blame him one bit. "The way I see it, you were either fucking around with my sister in the goddamn bathroom, or you're cheating on her. I don't know which is worse."

They glared at each other, anger rising. Faces inches apart, Gabe snarled, "Was. Amelia. In. The bathroom?"

* * * *

She was only seconds behind them, intent on following them to the basement when two small hands stopped her. "Amelia, when will the cookies be ready?" Camille wondered.

Her mother came around the counter, wiping her hands on a dishtowel. "What's going on?"

Amelia noticed then that everyone was watching her. Her mom seemed confused, her dad worried, and Grandma wore that same knowing smile she always did whenever Nick was involved. Her cousins didn't seem overly concerned with anything except chocolate chip cookies.

That's when they heard the first thump.

"Amelia, what's going on?" her mother demanded again.

"Come on, Sally," her father chided, "surely you've figured it out."

Amelia blushed. She struggled to find the words to put her mother at ease, but nothing came out.

Thud.

"You'd better get down there before they kill each other," her dad advised.

"Right." Amelia pushed everyone else from her mind and ran for the stairs.

So, now everyone knew. *Great.* She'd have to deal with that later. It was time to make Gabe give up this silly notion of protecting her.

In the heat of the moment, they mustn't have heard her footfalls on the stairs. Intent on giving them both a tongue-lashing, Amelia stopped short when she heard their argument.

"You fucking bastard!" Gabe shouted. Amelia was glad she'd shut the door behind her, the last thing Aunt Evelyn needed was her children using foul language learned from their cousin.

"I know. I know."

"What's changed? Why now?"

Amelia held her breath. Hidden in the stairwell, she hoped she might get the answers to the questions she'd been too scared to ask.

"Nothing. Nothing's changed."

"Something has to have changed."

The seconds ticked by without a response. Another thump shook the wall that veiled Amelia.

"If nothing's changed then what the hell happened three years ago?"

"Because of you!" Nick roared. "I just couldn't do that to

you."

"But now all of a sudden that doesn't matter anymore?" The gusto had disappeared from Gabe's voice.

"I couldn't walk away again. Not after the last time. It killed me. It just killed me to leave her like that. And then she hid away at school. I know what that did to you, and to your parents, and to her. I hated knowing that I'd been the cause. Then to make matters worse she started dating that jackass. To hell with it all, Gabe! To hell with you and your overprotective crap. I'm sick of it! Hate me if you want, but I'm not going to leave her again."

Amelia wanted to applaud. She crept down another step.

"I swear to god if you hurt her..."

"I won't."

"But if you do—"

"Gabe, I'm in love with her."

"What?" Amelia clapped a hand over her mouth, but she was too late. Her shocked gasp had already escaped.

Both Gabe and Nick cursed. They appeared at the bottom of the stairs. "Well this is just perfect," Nick grunted, but all Gabe could do was laugh. Amelia sat sheepishly on the steps.

"I told you all!" Grandma said from behind her. Amelia whipped around so fast she almost fell off the stairs. Nick reached out to steady her.

The landing at the top of the stairs was nearly overflowing with her family. "Nobody listens to a damn thing I say," Grandma kept rambling on. Amelia was mortified. Covering her face with her hands, she avoided looking at Nick. He grabbed her wrist and yanked her from the step.

"If you've all had your entertainment for the evening, this is really more of a private conversation." Nick stormed into the darkened basement, tugging her with him. "Come on."

"Dinner's in ten!" her mom called after them.

Still dumbfounded, Amelia let Nick lead her away from

her disbursing family.

He couldn't be serious about his admission. When he'd collared her two nights ago, she merely thought he'd been caught up in the game. Had he fallen in love with her? If so, when?

Each time she got an answer out of Nick, all she seemed to end up with was more questions.

Maybe he'd said it simply to shut Gabe up. His statement hadn't been meant for her ears, or her family's. A confession so large, particularly if it was false, could cause him to panic. What if he asked for the anklet back?

She was getting ahead of herself, but knowing that didn't stop the tears from blurring her vision.

Thrusting her into his bedroom, he shut the doors, eager to keep Gabe out. He sagged against them. "Well, this is just great."

Humour etched his voice, but it didn't put her at ease. Her sniffle drew his attention.

"You're upset. Why are you crying?"

She blinked back the tears. "I'm not."

He urged her to sit on the bed. Kneeling before her, he took her hands and kissed the knuckles. "Tell me what's wrong?"

"Were you making that stuff up?"

"You think I'm lying?" He was shocked. He reached for her foot and pulled on the chain. "What do you think this meant?"

She shrugged. She'd made assumptions about Nick in the past, and the truth had left her hollow, without hope.

He tugged on the chain. "I love you."

She wanted desperately to believe him. "Since when?"

Clasping her chin, he forced her to look at him. "Since always, Amelia. I *had* hoped to keep it from your family for a little longer, you know, maybe tell you first." He teased a smile from her. "I didn't mean to hurt you all those years ago, but I thought you were better off without me. Not to mention

I figured Gabe would probably put my nuts in a vice."

She giggled. "Probably."

"I'm sorry." He shifted to sit next to her. "I was going to wait until New Year's to ask you this, but I was wondering. Your dad's company is building my house. It'll be finished this spring."

"Yeah, he told me."

"Well, I was sort of wondering if you might stay there with me when it's done. It won't be until after you've graduated, but maybe you'd—"

"Nick, I'd love to."

A pent up breath came gushing from him.

"I spent the last few years trying to scrub you from my mind."

He winced. "I know. I'm glad you weren't totally successful."

"I wasn't successful at all. No matter what I tried. Three years ago I told you I loved you." Amelia picked at the polish on her fingernail. After everything they'd shared together over the past week, after all the things she'd let him do to her, opening up about her feelings still left her feeling exposed. "I still do."

Cupping her cheek, Nick forced her gaze to his. Leaning close, he kissed her. His confession, his tenderness, her own raw emotions consumed her. She closed her eyes and the tears slipped free. Bringing the kiss to an end, he rested his forehead against hers. Licking her lips, she tasted him there.

"I love you," he whispered.

She cracked a smile. "I love you, too."

He pushed up and offered her his hand. "We'd better get upstairs before Gabe shows up at this door, too."

She took his offered hand and he pulled her into his arms for another kiss, this one slightly longer, deeper. Leave it to Nick to increase her arousal with no intention of giving her relief.

Linking their fingers, he led her back through the basement. "I was thinking you might be interested in helping me decorate the house." He cast a wicked glance toward her before they ascended the stairs. "I'm very interested in hearing your suggestions on how we should furnish the basement."

Heart nearly bursting with joy, Amelia thought about their future. Oh, she had plenty of ideas.

About the Author

Romance author Cameron Allie grew up in a small town north of Toronto. As a child, she loved stories, and after reading her first romance novel at age fifteen her dreams of writing became singularly focused on the love story. She is currently living in Ontario with her husband, and with her cat, who is constantly trying to interrupt the writing process.

90400770R00108

Made in the USA
Middletown, DE
22 September 2018